Total-E-Bound Publishing books from AKM Miles:

Too Keen
Love, Jamie
Bought and Paid For

LOVE, GRANT

AKM MILES

Love, Grant
ISBN # 978-085715-072-1
©Copyright AKM Miles 2010
Cover Art by Natalie Winters ©Copyright 2010
Interior text design by Claire Siemaszkiewicz
Total-E-Bound Publishing

Published in 2010 by Total-E-Bound Publishing, Think Tank, Ruston Way, Lincoln, LN6 7FL, United Kingdom.

Total-E-Bound Publishing is an imprint of Total-E-Ntwined Limited.

Manufactured in the USA.

LOVE, GRANT

Dedication

This is dedicated to those who read my books and then write to let me know how they love the stories or characters and what the books mean to them. I am thrilled every time I hear from readers who like my work. It is very rewarding. So, this one goes out to the ones who've let me know I've made a good career choice. Every letter inspires me to write more. Thank you from the bottom of my heart. AKM

Chapter One

Jamie strode towards the bleachers on Field Nine, turning back to push the button on his remote keys to lock the truck door. Grant had bought the new Toyota Tacoma when he'd gotten his money from the insurance company after his accident last year. Jamie had really enjoyed the process as Grant had spent hours poring over web sites and information for weeks before deciding he would buy a 2009 white Tacoma with forty thousand miles on it.

Jamie had needed to work the morning that Grant had made the final decision based on what he could afford, not on what he really wanted. Still, it was exciting for Grant. Since he was going to be working at the Parks Department, a truck would come in handy. Remembering the call he'd gotten from Grant an hour after he'd gotten to work that day still made him smile.

"Oh my God, Jamie! You're not going to believe this. Wait 'til you see. I still can't believe it." Grant couldn't slow down long enough for Jamie to ask what in the world had him so freaked out.

"Hello? Wanna fill me in?" Jamie had finally gotten in.

"Oh, oh, sorry. I am *so* thrilled. What colour truck did I want?" Grant had paused waiting for Jamie to fill in the answer.

"Uh, silver."

"Yep. Twenty minutes before I got here this morning, a dealer from somewhere north of here showed up with the truck of my dreams, a 2011, silver Tacoma with less than three thousand miles on it. It has everything on it that I wanted. It was a dealer vehicle and guess what they wanted for it? Only three thousand more than the other one. I'm filling out the paperwork right now. I couldn't pass it up. Is that cool or what?"

"Oh, baby, that's more than cool. Two years newer, thirty-seven thousand less miles on it, the colour you wanted, and only three thousand more. This was meant to be. I'm so happy for you."

That had been a good day. Now Jamie was driving the Tacoma because his Taurus was in the shop. He might have to start looking for something new now that he had his PT license and was making more. He'd dropped Grant at work today and was coming now to catch the last of the games Grant was umpiring so he could take him home.

Jamie hurried to the field because he didn't want to miss any more of the game. He loved to watch Grant when he was umping. Grant was a different person on the field. Jamie had shown Grant many times how much it turned him on to see him out there.

Jamie liked coming to the park at night. The lights on the fields and the sounds of summertime and kids and competition made him happy. Families were everywhere, and it seemed like such a happy place. He could hear crowds on different fields yelling and encouraging players.

The crack of bats on balls from several games going on at the same time were like drumbeats marking the rhythm for the summer song. It could be chaotic but was really a well-scheduled plan that got great results for all the teams involved. He knew this because Grant had helped with it. As he headed up the bleachers, he heard his name called.

"Yo, Jamie, up here. Your boy's on tonight. He's puttin' on a show. I wonder if that's because he knew you'd be here to get him?" Tony, his neighbour and the county parks director, teased as Jamie sat down by him on the top bleacher.

"Shut up," Jamie said, playfully punching Tony's arm.

"Check it out, he's between second and third. This is an important game for the Raiders team, and the crowd is wild. He's pumped three out and flown four safe so far. Every time he does one, the crowd roars. It's like he's a star, and the crowd just waits for his performance. And it's cool, he doesn't do it every time. He saves it for the big plays. Hiring him was one of the best things I've done. Grant is so well-liked by workers, players, coaches, and, of course, the administration. Did you know he was getting a promotion?" Tony asked, watching Jamie to see if he was going to get to surprise him.

"No, I didn't. How come? Not that I don't think he deserves it. Lord, he's worked some long hours and done some hard work for the parks. Summertime is a killer, I know, but he comes home completely worn out. I'm just glad he's recovered so well from his injuries last year." Pretty much all of Grant's right side had been mangled in the wreck. A lot of good therapy had put Grant back into great shape.

"All right, look, here he goes, I bet. Watch. There's a player on first, and this batter that's up is known for bunts for some reason. I bet your guy's gonna show off, especially if he saw you come in." Tony pointed to the action on the field.

Jamie watched avidly as the play unfolded almost just as Tony predicted. His eyes were glued to Grant who was positioned just right to have a clear view of the play on second. Jamie loved the way Grant looked in his uniform. The tight, stretchy shorts let him move as he needed to, granted, but they were also beautifully form fitting. A couple of times, Grant had almost been late because he'd gotten tackled when Jamie saw him dressed up for his umpire duties.

Thunk! The ball was indeed rolling towards the pitcher who ran up for it. He scooped it from the ground, turned and slammed it towards the second baseman. The runner from first had already started for second when the ball was hit and was nearly there by the time the pitcher had the ball in hand.

The crowd was on its feet, and Jamie was yelling with the rest of them as the player slid into the base, right before the ball hit the second baseman's glove. Grant bent from the waist, spread his arms out and stood tall with them rising into what looked like bird wings.

"Safe!" And the crowd roared. Jamie and Tony turned to each other, laughing and punching the air as they watched lover and friend/employee respectively perform for the crowd. Grant, who was usually shy around people, very unassuming, seemed to become someone else when he was out there.

"He's having a ball. You know, he has another game to ump tonight, right? High school girls. It's another big one that will be crowded. I'm gonna stay and watch. There's been some trouble with one of the coaches. Grant can handle it, but I want to be here to back him up just in case something happens. Wanna get some food between the games, make a night of it?" Tony asked.

Tony, their neighbour, was one of Jamie and Grant's best friends and had been in the position of needing help in the parks system last summer when Grant needed a job. Grant had taken on more and more responsibilities as he'd become more a part of each area of the parks department.

Grant had taken classes in different aspects of the job he now held. It became obvious that he loved everything about working with the groups who used the county parks for so many activities. Jamie was glad he enjoyed his new career and was happy in it. That reminded him that Tony had said something about a promotion.

"Hey, what were you saying about a promotion for Grant? " Jamie asked Tony.

"Well, you know he's worked his way up to assistant to the assistant director. He was really overqualified for the menial work he started out doing. With all the extra work he's put in, the classes, the overtime, and so on, he's made an impression. I put his name in to take the current assistant, Barker's place. After the heart attack, Barker's decided to take it easy, take early retirement. That leaves the position open."

"Hmm, I wonder why he didn't say anything." Jamie looked out at Grant on the field.

"I can't say, but there aren't really any others who are as qualified for the position right now. It will have to be advertised, but I'll have final say. I'll be fair and give anyone who applies a chance, but I have to hand it to Grant. He's become pretty much irreplaceable with us. I'm pulling for him. Don't let him tell you he doesn't deserve it. He could do a lot for the department, and I'd promise him that he could still umpire at the night games."

Jamie laughed since he knew how much Grant enjoyed working with the young people. He'd often seen Grant answering questions with a group of players around him. Before the current game was over, Jamie got to see Grant do two outs and three other safes. The outs were spectacular.

Grant would drop down on one knee, the left one, putting his other leg out straight. His left arm would go out straight to the front and the right fist would start at the about wrist level of the left arm and pump back and forth about five times, hard and fast, and Grant would let out this yell that could be heard three fields over, "*You'r-r-r-r-r-r-re out!*"

It had gotten to where fans in the stands would do the pumping motion with Grant. Jamie's heart thumped every time he saw it. Grant was so intensely in the moment.

After the game, Jamie hurried down to the field and was there when Grant came off, sweaty and dirty, and sexy as hell. He knew better than to get too close or he'd be tempted to touch, and he didn't want to embarrass Grant by making any gestures that would make him have to hide anything that came up. He high-fived Grant as soon as he got near him.

"Hey, I'm glad you made it. Gosh, it's hot. July's gonna be worse." Grant smiled with his lush lips and those gorgeous eyes, and Jamie's heart beat triple time. Grant was so in love with him that it just shone from his eyes, and that made Jamie's whole world. It's a wonder everyone couldn't see how they felt about each other. Jamie was sure his eyes revealed the same level of devotion.

"I'm the one with the regular hours, remember? That means I get to come and watch your show," Jamie teased.

"It's not my show. It's the kids'." Grant ducked his head. He performed out there but was then embarrassed when anyone mentioned how cool it was.

"Okay, I'll quit. It's a girl's game next, right? I'm staying with Tony. We were going to get something to eat. Want me to wait and eat with you, or did you get to have something earlier?" Jamie asked.

"Nah, go ahead. I had a salad someone brought in before the game. I see Tony getting food. Go on and eat with him. I'll see you later. Man, I'm glad it's Saturday night. We can both sleep a little late tomorrow." Grant looked tired to Jamie.

"And it means we can have a shower, a massage, and play for a while tonight," Jamie leant in to say, before he turned to walk off. He knew if he looked at Grant after that remark, they'd get caught up in looking at each other, and those who didn't see them making goo-goo eyes at each other would surely see the hard-on each sported at thinking about what would happen later.

Jamie swore he heard Grant mutter, "Payback!" before he got too far away. He smiled, looking forward to making restitution for the evil trick he'd just played.

Grant Stevens watched Jamie walk away and wondered if he'd ever lose the feeling of wonder at how happy he was and how much he loved Jamie Taylor. His horrible accident last year had not been a good thing, but what came from it certainly had been. Jamie had been a tech at the rehab centre then, and as a big, strong man, he'd spent a lot of time helping with Grant, also a big man, who'd been unable to do much for himself for a good while.

As the players left the field, gathered their equipment, met their parents, and headed out, the other team began setting up for their game. Grant used the free time to watch Jamie, a favourite pastime. Jamie wore what Grant loved to see him in — tight light blue jeans and a plaid cotton shirt with the sleeves cut out. To Grant, he looked good enough to eat. He had to stop himself from licking his lips.

"Mr. Stevens, can I ask you for a favour?"

Grant turned at the question and saw a teenager with a Raiders fan T-shirt on. She was a cute girl, the sister of one of the players, and Grant had seen her here before. She was always kind and very polite, always thanking him for his work, something that never occurred to most teens. Actually, not many adults bothered to mention it either, he thought.

"If I can, Janet. What do you need?" He couldn't imagine what he could possibly do for the bright, pony-tailed blonde.

"We're having a sort of carnival thing before the state tournament to make money for the team. There's gonna be a Dunk-a-Hunk booth. Would you, I mean, will you come and sit in it for a half hour for us? A bunch of us think a lot of people would pay to... I mean, not that you're not fair, but... Oh, gosh," Janet said, blushing now. "We all think you're a hunk."

Grant burst out laughing at the idea of a teen-aged girl, or a bunch of them, thinking he was a hunk. But he would be glad to help them.

"I tell you what, if it doesn't interfere with my job, I'll be glad to show up and let people throw balls at me and try to get me back a little. I'll even see if I can bring someone else with me, and I'll get him to promise you a half hour, too. How's that?"

"Cool. Is he a hunk, too?"

Grant looked over to where Tony and Jamie were getting their food from the concession stand. He pointed to Jamie and said, "See the guy in the plaid shirt and blue jeans?"

"Gosh, he's hot. Oh my God, you can get him? We've seen him here before. Wait'll I tell Melanie. She'll freak. Please, if you can both come that would be all I'm supposed to come up with, and I'll have the best hunks there. I'll be a star." Janet sounded as if she'd won the lottery.

"I can't promise, but if we're both free from work at that time, we'll both be there. Just let me know when and where," Grant said, patting her on the shoulder.

She squealed and ran off to another girl, and after speaking to her with much pointing to both Jamie and him, they both squealed, causing several people to turn and look. Grant turned away quickly. Okay, enough of that. Grabbing a bottle of water, he took a big swig then chucked it back towards his duffel. He snuck another quick look at Jamie and sighed at his good fortune. How that man had changed his life.

When Grant had met Jamie last year, he'd been so far in the closet he'd not recognised, at first, what the attraction he felt for Jamie was all about. It didn't take long to figure things out. They were mutually smitten, and the relationship progressed quickly. Yeah, he thought, quickly, but not smoothly. He spared a thought for the nutcase who'd terrorised them due to his jealousy over Jamie. Donnie Wilkins, the rehab centre director's son, had a thing for Jamie, totally unrequited. When Grant had shown up and Jamie had showed an interest in him, Donnie had lost it.

Donnie had made his anger known in several ways, all increasingly scary and destructive. Grant shivered as he remembered Donnie poisoning Jamie's beloved dog, Brit. Luckily, Brit had pulled through, as did Miss Wilhemina, one of Jamie's LOL's, little old ladies, from the centre, who Donnie had tried to smother with a pillow. Donnie was out to hurt anything and anyone Jamie loved.

After several incidents, and with the police unable to locate Donnie, he and Jamie had ended it by setting up Donnie. It had gone horribly wrong, and for a while, it had looked like Donnie might actually kill Grant in order to have Jamie for himself. Now Donnie was living off the government in a prison in a neighbouring state, thank God. It would be a long time before he saw the outside again. Since Donnie's arrest and imprisonment, Grant and Jamie had been unbelievably happy.

Jamie had gone on and finished the courses he'd been working on in physical therapy and was still working at the centre, but now he had a much better job. He still checked on his little old ladies, though. Everyone loved Jamie. He exuded such compassion and encouragement and true kindness that he was a real asset to the place. Grant knew Jamie loved his work with the people there and he, personally, knew how good he was at his job.

They'd already admitted to having feelings for each other by the time Jamie invited Grant to his house to stay in his guest room while he continued his outpatient therapy, since this wasn't Grant's home town. Grant had taken him up on it, but he'd never used the guest room.

Grant was so happy doing what he was now that he didn't miss the old coaching job he'd had before the accident. He loved Jamie, Brit, the house, the neighbours and the new job. He couldn't be happier. He heard a whistle he recognised as Jamie's and looked up to see him returning to his seat with Tony. Jamie winked at him and put a little shimmy in his walk as he mounted the steps.

Payback, I'm telling you, Grant thought.

Grant turned back to the field and set about his duties with the new teams and coaches.

Great, he thought, *motor mouth.* He dreaded working with the coach for the visiting team. The big man had a bad habit of cursing at the girls on the team, as well as ridiculing them when they made mistakes. Grant didn't believe in either of those things and had cautioned him about it more than once. Now, the coach had a pretty good-sized chip on his shoulder when it came to Grant. He pushed just a little more each time they crossed paths. Grant was determined to be professional in his dealings with the man, but he was not going to let him get by with that behaviour, either.

When all the preliminaries were over, he yelled, "Play ball!" and it was on.

The game moved fast for the first three innings, and he felt as if it would be an okay night. One girl, in left field, was a bit larger than most of the others, and she was a little slow. A couple of times, he'd seen the coach jump up and yell when she missed a ball or didn't get it back in quick enough, but it hadn't been worth making a scene over.

Grant paid close attention because of the coach's actions, so he knew to be watching her. The girl, Alison, messed up another play. She'd tried hard to make the catch but tripped just before she caught it. It was clear she wasn't hurt as she rolled right back up, but she had to run over and retrieve the ball and was late getting it infield. The runner crossed home a good bit before the ball made the catcher's mitt. Grant spied the coach coming out of the dugout and onto the field, yelling at the girl.

Sparing a quick glance to make sure Alison was all right, he turned back to see the Coach, Gilbert, was in the middle of the diamond, and his language belonged in a bar, not on a playing field with a group of young girls.

"You fat bitch, I've told you if you messed up again, I'd throw you off the team. I should've never allowed you on the field. Need to have my head examined. Don't duck your head, you big wimp. I'm sick of your tears and excuses. Damn it, I've had it with this shit. Come over here. You know what you deserve now so—"

Grant wasn't having it. "Coach Gilbert, stop right there. Sir, I'm asking you to walk back off this field, and I want no more of that language in front of these young women and the kids in the stands. Go back, now, sir." Grant pointed to the dugout and hoped the angry coach would obey.

"You stay out of this, pretty boy. You've missed three fucking calls tonight, dumbass, and you have no business telling me how to handle my players. Come on, Fat Al, you heard me. Move it, Fatso." The girl's tears and fear were egging him on. It sickened Grant to see the humiliation he caused.

The coach started for Alison, and Grant planted himself between the coach and player before he said, "Coach Gilbert, you're out of the game. Leave the field, gather your things, and leave the dugout. I've warned you about your language and your treatment of your players. Now, sir. Don't make me have to tell you again." Grant hated the way this was turning into a scene. Everyone stood still watching the exchange. The crowd was silent, and he wondered if Tony would back him up if it came down to it.

Coach Gilbert looked from Grant to Alison to the rest of his team, and he must have decided to push it. He walked over to Grant and with a stiff finger, he poked Grant in the chest as he said, "Motherfucker, you can't throw me out of the game. You're just some pissant employee here who doesn't know his ass from his elbow. I'm not—"

"Get your hand off me this instant, or I'll throw you out of the park. Now, back off." Grant was deadly serious now, and he knew he'd be within his rights to send the coach packing.

"You and whose army? You're just a little too big for your britches, aren't you, boy?" Coach Gilbert prodded him, leaning in almost close enough to spit on Grant as he talked. And his finger still poked Grant's chest.

Grant put one hand up high, fingers wide and dropped one finger at a time until none were left, and when he finished his silent countdown, he said, in a booming voice, "You're. Out. Of. The. *Park!*"

His index finger popped back up, and he pointed to the entrance to the park. He began to move forward, crowding the coach and making him walk backward. Grant nearly laughed when the sputtering coach tripped over the pitcher's mound and nearly went down. Grant kept it up until they were at the team's dugout. Again, he pointed, this time to the coach's belongings then stood with arms crossed. The coach turned back to him as if to argue more.

"You are forfeiting this game. You want to make it another one? You're out for one year. I'm counting to ten, and you'd better be in your car and on your way by the time I get there. One..." Grant held up one finger, again over his head, and the crowd took up the count with him as each finger went up. "Two...three..." Now the spectators were clapping as they counted to ten.

Grant felt sick as the coach kept sending him glances filled with hatred. He stomped around, grabbed his stuff and headed to his car quickly. By the time his car started and he roared off, the crowd was cheering in support of Grant's punishment.

He turned to the girls on the team and said, "I'm sorry, girls, but that is totally inappropriate. You're out this one game. Maybe you can make it up later. Your assistant coach can take over. Is there a problem with anyone here?" he asked, looking at the expectant faces.

Alison stepped up and spoke for all of them, "No sir. We appreciate what you did. I do, I mean. Thank you." As she finished, the other girls all nodded and muttered agreement. He heard murmurs of 'tired', 'scared', 'mean' and 'finally'.

Grant turned now to look for Tony and see if he was in trouble for his actions. Tony raised one hand with the thumb up. Jamie held up one hand with the sign language symbol for *I love you* on it. Thumb and pinkie spread wide, index finger up, other fingers curved down. It was a cross between I which is just the pinkie up, Love which is the classic L symbol you see on people's forehead when they're saying Loser...mixed with the pinkie and the thumb out for Y or for You. The three signs mixed together meant I love you. Jamie flashed it at Grant while Grant was looking up at the top bleacher at both of them. Grant could see that Jamie's other hand was still clenched in a fist. He figured it was a good thing Coach Gilbert was leaving the park.

With the game over early, everyone scattered off the bleachers, parents went over to their kids and gathering equipment. Several of them stopped to thank Grant for what he'd done. He wasn't proud, but he knew he'd been right. A sports event was not the right place for bullies and mistreatment of young people who were just learning how to play the game and understand what sportsmanship was about. Neither could he allow the man to thwart his authority during a game.

Frankly, his stomach was beginning to quiver and, as the adrenaline started wearing off, he wished he could just be somewhere quiet, preferably with Jamie. He looked up as he heard his name called. It was Tony.

"Relax. Take the deer in the headlights look off your face. You did the right thing, Grant. He's been asking for just that. Any number of the things he did tonight could have gotten him thrown out. You took more than I would. You'll have no problem from this. I'm behind you on it. I'm going to finish up here. You go now. I think someone is waiting for you at the truck." Tony slapped him on the back and pushed him in the direction of the parking lot.

"Thanks, man. I'll do a report on it tomorrow. I promise." That's all Grant could get out. His eyes smarted, and he didn't want anyone to see that the whole ordeal had rattled him. He stopped to pick up his duffel bag and headed out. As soon as he got to the parking lot, his Tacoma pulled up and the door opened as if by magic. A haven...with an angel right there, waiting for him.

Jamie motioned for him to hop in, and Grant pitched his duffel in the back then climbed in, slamming the door, taking an odd satisfaction in the sound. More contentment came from the open hand that was waiting for his on the console. Grant slipped his fingers through Jamie's and squeezed, showing his gratitude for the quick pick up and the ready support.

Grant was sure that Jamie knew what Grant needed right now, and he let Jamie go about providing it. It was nice knowing that someone knew you so well that words weren't necessary. Grant knew they'd talk it over and hash it out and get the anger and frustration and feelings out, but right now, Grant needed quiet and…ice cream?

Jamie pulled into the Dairy Queen and ordered for both of them. With dessert therapy in hand, Jamie drove out to one of the other parks, a more remote one that was further out in the country and pulled up behind a set of bleachers. The park was empty and the lights weren't even on, except for a few security ones far from where they were.

"Thanks, Jamie."

"I've got your back, Grant. We'll talk in a minute. Maybe walk around a little out there." Jamie pointed to a couple of older ball fields that were seldom used anymore, with all the newer parks closer to town. Jamie knew Grant liked this old park, and they'd been here before a couple of time before — once to let Grant drive around the different paths while getting used to driving again. The other time was a more sensual memory. While Grant scooped up little bites of his Oreo Cookie Blizzard, he remembered the time he and Jamie had taken a blanket and made love on the outfield of the farthest ball field in the deserted park.

Chapter Two

"Are we crazy?" Grant had asked as that night as he'd walked with Jamie, holding his hand and clutching the bag with the 'stuff' in it. They had bottled water, washcloths, lube, condoms and candy bars.

"Yeah, but doesn't it feel great? You're sure no one comes out here, right? Like, ever?"

"Nah, I've done rounds several times, and there's never anyone here after lights out."

"So will someone be doing rounds checking it out tonight?"

"Yeah."

"Grant!"

"Me. I said I'd take it tonight, silly. You think I'd take a chance with getting caught? I'm all for a little adventure, but I'm not into public displays. Here's good," Grant said, stopping and setting the bag down. He stood by while Jamie spread out the old quilt from the back of the car. Jamie turned from his task and opened his arms. Grant went into them with a laugh that turned into a moan.

"I know you wouldn't take any chances. Come here with those lips." Jamie took Grant's mouth without their usual preliminaries. A lot of the time, their kisses were truly like building a work of art. Whoever started it would begin with soft licks and nibbles of the other's lips, teasing and tasting. Tongues would meet and tangle, usually slowly at first before becoming more aggressive. Seldom did they stay soft and sweet for too long. Jamie usually caved first and began thrusting his tongue into Grant's mouth, eagerness and desire evident in his moans and sighs. Grant was quick to reciprocate with his own moves, either sucking on Jamie's tongue or chasing it back into his mouth and following Jamie's precedent.

Of course, those kisses usually led to more lovemaking. Tonight, Jamie was changing it up a little, Grant realised as his mouth was forced open and Jamie's tongue swept in, thrusting immediately, as if Jamie had passed over the first steps and was moving headlong into passion. Grant met Jamie's need with a matching frenzy. However Jamie came at him, Grant was always ready to participate.

"God, you're hot tonight," Grant said, tightening his arms around Jamie.

"Hot for you. I thought about you all day. I can't believe you came up with this. We're really gonna get nekkid out here?" Jamie teased him.

"Right now." Grant pulled back and started unbuttoning his shirt, pulling it out of his jeans. At the same time, he toed off his sneakers without untying them. Before long, he was kicking his jeans and underwear off together, and he stood before Jamie, proud and eager.

"My God, you are such a fucking gift." Jamie never took his eyes off Grant as he undressed as fast as he could.

"I'm not a gift, Jamie. I'm a man in love, and one who's getting pretty anxious to not be the only one naked out here." Grant felt a little exposed with Jamie watching him like that and slowing down with his disrobing while he gazed at Grant's body.

"Jamie, uh, now?" Grant started to turn to settle down onto the quilt. Over the last year, since he'd come out of the closet and admitted he was gay after meeting Jamie, Grant had experienced many firsts. That didn't mean he was totally comfortable with being...oh shit!

Jamie had dropped to his knees as soon as he dropped the last bit of clothing, and the next thing Grant knew, Jamie had taken his cock into his hand, drawing it into the heat of his mouth.

"Ah! Jamie, God. I can't believe you. Oh, oh, that's..." Grant could talk no more. His hands moved down to hold onto Jamie's head, and he moved his fingers through Jamie's hair. Jamie moved his head back and forth, providing wet suction and proving he was serious about making this new experience one Grant would remember. Getting a blowjob wasn't new to Grant. But having said blowjob outside—and not outside within the privacy of their solidly fenced in backyard—was definitely very new.

"Jamie, oh, love you so much. I'm not sure I can stand much longer. Oh!" Jamie had moved his other hand to Grant's balls and rolled them in their sac. Grant groaned and felt fire race up his spine then back down to settle in his balls. He couldn't control it anymore. Jamie pulled back enough to swallow Grant's cum. He took a few moments to clean Grant then wrapped his arms around Grant's hips to ease him down to the quilt.

"Good Lord, Jamie, that was unbelievable. I kind of had planned to make love to you tonight. Just so you know, not complaining here." Grant rolled down and pulled Jamie with him. He planned on making good on his earlier plans. A change in the order of things might be called for, but he could work with that. Grant kept rolling until Jamie was under him and he leant down to put his lips to Jamie's.

In this kiss, he followed Jamie's lead and bypassed gentle and went straight for passion. His tongue invaded and moved through Jamie's mouth, looking for taste, texture, and participation. Jamie met him in the game, and they thrust and parried like the best of fencers, and Grant was delighted with the deep breaths Jamie was forced to take as need grew from their involvement. Exciting Jamie was something he loved above all else. When he'd fallen in love, he'd embraced the life and its joys fully.

"Damn, Grant, you're hot tonight. What's gotten into you? No, wait, I don't care. I love it. Love you, don't stop." Jamie opened again and went right back to sucking on the tongue that was right there. Grant couldn't get enough of Jamie. As a matter of fact…

"I want you, right here, right now," Grant murmured, as he slid his mouth across Jamie's cheek to his ear, taking in and biting the lobe, easing it with a swipe of his tongue.

"Jesus, Grant. You got me. How do you want it? I'm all yours." Jamie took Grant's hand and put it on his cock, hard and leaking. Jamie thrust up a couple of times and Grant got the message. He moved down Jamie's torso, taking just a little time to pay tribute to favourite spots with nips and licks. Soon his mouth and his hand were working over Jamie's cock, and he liked the sounds he heard over his head. Jamie squirmed and bucked under him, but Grant didn't budge. He was determined to do this for Jamie then he was going to do Jamie, for himself.

He applied himself with single-minded determination and soon had the results he was working towards. Jamie gasped, groaned, and shot hard deep into Grant's throat. Grant swallowed him down and took the time to clean up and make sure Jamie was completely free of any of the sticky residue from his release.

Grant looked up at Jamie, the little light available from a nearly full moon and the distant security lights just letting him see the sleepy-sexy look in his lover's eyes. That's what he'd been going for. He raised up and crawled up Jamie's body, straddling his as he did. He settled with his hips over Jamie's, letting balls and cocks settle together in a comfortable mesh, like jigsaw pieces. Leaning over, he put his hands on the quilt beside Jamie's head and leaned to put his face right above Jamie's.

"Uh, hi," Jamie said, watching Grant closely, as if to see just what he had in mind next.

"Hi, yourself, gorgeous. You asked how I wanted you before. I want you like this. I want to look down at this face that makes me happy. I want to watch you lose it when I come inside you. I want to make you go crazy and beg me to never stop."

Jamie shivered, and Grant saw goose bumps appear on his skin. Gratifying, that.

"God, Grant, I don't know what's got hold of you tonight, but I love it. I'm already of a mind to beg. Take me. Now, please." Jamie raised his hips, pushing up against Grant, making all kinds of good connections.

Grant pressed right back, mashing their groins together in exquisite contact. He reached for the bag with the lube and condoms, snagging the cloth at the same time. He'd planned well, as the cloth was damp inside a zippered bag. They both knew they were safe and could bareback if they wanted and probably would at some point, but they both agreed that for right now, at least, they would continue with the rubbers. Deadly diseases weren't the only reasons for being careful. Neither wanted to worry about infections or other possible problems. One of these days, though, it would be what they both wanted badly enough and it would have great meaning.

"Get me ready? And I'll return the favour," Grant suggested. He gave Jamie the condom and lube and tried to hold still as Jamie covered him, then slathered his cock before handing the lube to Grant. Scooting down a little, he put his knees between Jamie's legs and spread them while covering his fingers with lube. He bent to his task, reaching with one hand to spread Jamie. With the other, he made sure both the inside and out of Jamie's hole was prepared for him to enter. Wanting this to go as smoothly as possible, Grant teased and stretched at the same time, making Jamie squirm and push, trying to get more of Grant inside him.

Deeming Jamie ready, Grant moved his fingers aside, holding the other cheek now. He placed his cock at Jamie's entrance and looked up so he could watch Jamie's face as he pushed inside. Ah, Grant didn't know what he liked more, the intensity of pleasure that spread through him as he was enveloped in tightness and heat, or the look of utter bliss and unconditional love on Jamie's face. Jamie brought his arms down and hooked them behind his knees, pulling them up towards his chest, letting Grant in further and with more ease. Grant began to rock.

With Jamie spread wide and open like that, Grant was able to pause and lean down to thrust his tongue in Jamie's mouth and mock the motion from below. Jamie let out a sound that was a cross between a grunt and a whimper that Grant relished. He couldn't help it. Many times, he'd been in just the position Jamie was in, and he knew how it felt to be so filled and what the force of the feelings in both body and soul did to him. Jamie was flying now, looking as if he could just soar with the feelings he was experiencing and Grant was right with him, with the added bonus of knowing he'd done that for Jamie.

Rising back up, Grant began to pump hard and fast, making sure he touched Jamie's prostate often, making Jamie's breath gust out in loud bursts. Unable to sustain that for very long, Grant looked at Jamie and smiled, winked then rammed in as hard as he could, coming nearly as hard. He jerked and groaned as he filled the condom. Gathering his scattered wits about him, he reached down and started pulling on Jamie's cock. It didn't take more than a couple of slides of his fist. Grant thought surely Jamie's scream would bring the woodland animals out to see what had been treed. Spurts of cum flew up and hit Jamie's stomach, chest, and even his chin.

Carefully, Grant pulled out and disposed of the condom in the same zippered bag that the cloth came from. He cleaned himself and Jamie then replaced it and zipped it away, feeling like Harry Homemaker as he did. He pitched it over by the bag then reached for the bottle of water. He sucked down a big drink then reached out to take Jamie's hand, pulling him so he could sit up. Jamie drank, too, and Grant put the water away. He moved so his legs went around Jamie's waist and sat in his lap now, arms and legs wrapped around him. Their faces were about an inch apart.

"Hi," Grant whispered.

"Hi, indeed. What have you got to say for yourself?" Jamie teased.

"I love you. I wanted to show you how much."

"I have to be the luckiest man alive." Jamie's eyes moved back and forth between Grant's eyes and his mouth.

"No, that's the man you live with," Grant assured him.

Jamie leaned that little bit and touched Grant's lips and now the kiss was soft and slow.

Grant sighed as he participated in the sweetness Jamie offered. Tongues came out to play, but gently, with little touches and glides that had hearts hammering, not in passion as before but in grateful harmony —

"You know," Jamie asked into the silence interrupting Grant's memory of that night. "It was all I could do not to come off those bleachers tonight," Jamie said, into the silence.

Grant snapped out of his reverie and turned his head. "Were you afraid I couldn't handle it?" he asked, putting the empty ice cream cup into the bag Jamie always asked for when they got ice cream. Jamie added his, and Grant tied it up.

"Not in the least," Jamie said with a snort. "I just wanted to back you up. I had even taken a step when Tony grabbed my arm. When that asshole put his hand on you, I wanted to jump in. But damn, Grant, you were great. Impressively calm, but no one doubted you were a badass out there. When you put that hand up and counted him down before you threw him out, I had the biggest hard-on ever watching my man. I was so proud of you, babe. He was a weasel."

"I just had to get him off the field. He was really going after that girl, Alison. She didn't deserve that. That's not what sports are about," Grant said.

"Tony said there might be trouble with him. He stayed to back you up, too. I doubt if he was as turned on as I was by watching you, though, thank heaven! You were a sight out there, and you had the crowd with you. They didn't like the way he was acting either." Jamie shook his head, clearly remembering the incident and how it went down.

"I've known coaches like him before, in basketball. Ones who get off on yelling and making a big scene, never thinking about how their behaviour was affecting the minds of the young people they're supposed to be teaching. They should be teaching fundamentals and sportsmanship." Grant hated to sound bitter, but it really bothered him when people abused positions of authority.

"Well, you're teaching them the right way, and you were very exciting and sexy out there tonight," Jamie said, turning as much as he could with the steering wheel in the way, and reaching out for Grant's face.

"I bet you're the only one who thought I was sexy," Grant said, leaning in to accept the caress Jamie offered.

"Bet I'm not. Half the girls think you're hot stuff," Jamie teased. "They just don't know you're mine." Now Jamie leant over the console and slid his hand behind Grant's head to pull him in for a kiss.

"Uh, speaking of hot stuff…" Grant tried to say, but Jamie wasn't through with his lips yet. Grant put his hand behind Jamie's head and held on, letting the kiss take his mind off the night's troubles and into the more immediate joys to be experienced.

"Mmm, okay, speaking of…you were saying?" Jamie pulled away, licking his lips, making Grant smile.

"I sort of obligated you to help out at a carnival they're having for the Raiders team to make enough money to go to state competition this year," Grant said.

"Okay. What's that got to do with you being hot stuff?" Jamie tilted his head, looking at Grant with an expression that was adorable. Okay, maybe it was adorable only to him, but it made his heart thud and his toes curl. Hot stuff, indeed.

"One of the girls asked if I'd take a half hour in the Dunk-a-Hunk booth, and I told her I'd try to get you to do a stint in there, too. I hope that was okay. She was thrilled when I pointed you out, by the way." Grant laughed at Jamie's raised eyebrows.

"Oh God, coveted by teenage girls. Scary." Jamie laughed, but said, "Of course, I'll help, especially if you're there. We could have fun at a carnival together."

"No doubt. I could have fun with you no matter where we were," Grant admitted.

"Back at you, babe. You want to walk around out here or are you ready to go home? You know, where there's a shower and a bed and a happy pup waiting for some loving? Oh yeah, and me, also waiting for some loving."

"I'll take 'home', Alex, for two hundred," Grant said, and laughed with Jamie. He'd had to watch a lot of TV for a while last year when he was recuperating, and Jeopardy was something they sometimes watched together, laughing at how much they didn't know, but being surprised often, too, at how much they did.

* * * *

Much later that night, clean, massaged into pure relaxation then loved into total oblivion, Grant hovered on the brink of sleep, his limbs entwined with Jamie's when he heard Jamie whisper, "You asleep?"

"Nope."

"Why didn't you tell me that you were up for promotion?" Jamie asked, sounding curious and a little hurt. Maybe that last was just in Grant's mind.

"I hadn't really processed it yet. It's not for sure. They've got to advertise it, and I'm sure there's someone out there a lot more qualified. Tony just mentioned it in passing, and frankly, I didn't pay it much attention," Grant said, wanting Jamie to know he'd never leave him out if he thought it was something important.

"Oh, okay."

"Hey, I'd have told you if I thought it would really happen. It would be a good increase in pay, but a whole lot more responsibility, too. I would definitely discuss it with you before I made a decision like that—one that would affect us both." Grant pushed up on his hand, so he could look down at Jamie in the faint light from the digital clock on the radio by the bed. The blue colour made it seem strangely eerie in the middle of the night.

"It's okay. My feelings aren't hurt or anything, but Tony sounded like he thought you were qualified and that he was going to push for you to get it, even though he'd have to interview if someone else applied."

"I don't want him giving me any special treatment," Grant knew he sounded dismayed, thinking Tony might used their friendship like that and maybe get in trouble for it later.

"Don't worry about it, Grant. He said he'd be fair and look at anyone who applied. He's not going to be anything but honest, you know that," Jamie said, pulling Grant back down to his shoulder.

"Yeah, you're right," Grant said, yawning.

He was nearly back to oblivion when Brit jumped up from the corner, barked loudly and went flying to the back door, growling and scratching — something Brit *never* did. Both Jamie and Grant jumped as if they'd heard shots fired. They grabbed shorts and were close behind Brit.

"What the hell?" Jamie asked.

"What's up, I wonder? You reckon it's an animal? Raccoon or something?" Grant suggested.

By now they were at the back door where Brit was still going crazy, wanting out and sounding mad about it. Grant was a little worried about Jamie letting him out there.

"That sounds like anger, not curiosity," Grant said, watching as Jamie tried to peer outside. He reached to open the door, and Brit was out and gone. They both followed onto the patio and watched as Brit headed straight for the back fence. He stopped at one spot, right under the area where the neighbour's tree limb provided shade for their yard and barked and pawed and whined.

"He must have smelled some animal. Damn! That scared me spitless. That's the first time he's done that since, uh, since last year," Grant said.

Jamie whistled for Brit, who ignored him. That, too, wasn't like Brit.

"Brit, come back here, boy. You're going to wake the whole neighbourhood." He whistled again and Grant watched as Brit turned to look at them as if to say, "Are you crazy?" The dog turned back to the fence and growled one more time before heading in. When he got back to them, he whined and rubbed up against first Jamie then Grant. It was almost as if he'd been scared and was looking for reassurance. It was very weird.

"Hey, boy, what was it? You protecting us from a big, bad squirrel? Or was it a racoon? Maybe an opossum? Come on, I'll give you a treat, my good guard dog. Let's go in before someone calls the cops for all the noise." Jamie herded them back inside where he made good on his promise, giving Brit one of his favourite treats.

At first, Grant thought Brit wasn't going to take it. He just looked at Jamie, who stood with his hand out, a puzzled look on his face. Brit went to the door, gave one more bark and growl, came back and took the treat then headed for the bedroom.

"Is it just me, or was that the weirdest thing ever?" Jamie looked at Grant.

"Not just you, man. That was totally out there. It was like he was saying, 'Guys, you're not listening to me, but fine, if you want to ignore me, I'll take your treat'."

"I felt the same thing. Dang, let's go try to get some sleep. I was just about gone when he freaked," Jamie said, taking Grant's hand and pulling him towards the bedroom.

"Me, too. Sounds good," Grant said, putting an arm around Jamie as they neared the bed. They stopped and looked. Brit was on the bed. Brit was never on the bed.

"Too fucking weird," Jamie said, looking from Brit to Grant. "Brit, what's going on? You know you don't sleep on the bed. Get down now," Jamie pointed to the dog's bed in the corner.

Brit barked once and put his head down on his paws. He scooted down a little so he was at the very foot of the bed, but he didn't get down.

"Brit!" Jamie tried to sound authoritative as he pointed to the corner again. Brit whined and raised his head before dropping it one more time.

"Jamie? He's seriously freaked about something. It is a big bed…" Grant said.

"You don't think he'll take advantage and want to sleep with us all the time? I don't want to start something we can't stop," Jamie said, looking puzzled.

"No, I really think this is a one-time thing. Come on, he's never tried it before. Let's just get some sleep," Grant begged, for both Brit and himself.

"Fine. Come on."

* * * *

Oh, if they only knew. The figure hidden behind the fence was all but rubbing his hands with glee. If those two knew what was about to happen, their blood would run cold in their veins.

Donnie Wilkins had learned a lot in the last year, planning, cunning, how to work the system to get what he wanted, and the importance of patience. He was going to enjoy toying with those two before he killed them both. His once-felt infatuation with Jamie had turned to bitterness. Now he just wanted revenge on both of them. He'd get it, too.

He thought about the meeting he'd had just that day with his parole officer.

"Yes, sir. The job is going very well. Mr. Ragan is good to me. He doesn't harp on the fact that I'm ex-con. I don't mind the work at all. I always liked working on cars, and I pretty much stay in the back of the shop. It's all good." Donnie had put the right amount of humility in his voice. It wasn't really hard to work people when you knew what the end result would be.

"No problems where you're living?" the bored man had asked. Officer Gann was a retired policeman who now sat behind a desk and flapped his jaws all day. He was a nobody.

"No, sir, none. It's not much, but I can afford it, and I don't need much. It came furnished, and even though it's small, I'm fine there." Hell, the place was a dump, and he hated it, but nothing mattered but his plan. He could sleep anywhere. He'd proven that, hadn't he?

"What about the counselling? Are you set up and going to those meetings?" Officer Gann asked, stifling a yawn.

"I've been to one. I think they're going to help a lot, sir." Shit. A total waste of time. He'd sat through the damn thing, silent and still, using the time to mentally go through his plan in his head.

"Well, William. Everything seems to be in order. I'll see you next week, same time. Stay clean, okay?" This was said without the man even raising his head to look at Donnie. Not that Donnie cared. He wanted to be invisible.

As he'd walked away from the meeting earlier today, he'd been shaking. Talking to anyone about where he'd been brought it all back. Prison was forty kinds o' hell. Donnie Wilkins had always considered himself to be pretty much a bad ass. Finding out early in lock up that he was a shaking, crying, scared little shit was demoralising and life changing.

Donnie had spent half of the last year piss-in-his-pants scared. He doubted if he'd slept one night through the whole time he'd been in. All those things he'd heard about what happened to new guys in prison. All true. Shit. The first six months or so he'd been a snivelling, whining, wimp, one that delighted the stronger, meaner inmates.

And there was always someone stronger and meaner. He'd learned that.

Finding out this about himself had bred such a hate for the two men who had caused his stay there that he'd finally become strong himself. He'd come to the conclusion that he could continue as he was or he could become one of the chosen, as he thought of them. That was what started the planning and patience lessons. While he'd worked out how he was going to get back at Jamie Taylor and Grant Stevens, he'd been lucky enough to be in the right place at the right time.

Mop in hand, Donnie had been in the last stall in the bathroom when he heard two men talking. Recognising one of his tormentors, he'd frozen, praying they wouldn't find him. Thinking they were alone, they'd talked freely, and his future was set.

"When?"

"Tomorrow night, at last guard change. All three are going down at the same time." Donnie had heard a scraping noise. A switchblade? How had someone gotten a switchblade in here? But he knew the sound well. He'd held his breath, hoping for more. An idea had already been forming in his mind.

"How we gonna get away with it?" That was Harlon. The first one was Quint. Bastard. He'd made Donnie's life hell, in so many humiliating ways. Fucking pervert. The fact that Donnie had thought about doing the same type thing with Jamie was beside the point. Donnie's whole perception of what happened between two men had been bastardised. He no longer wanted Jamie for his own. He wanted Jamie and Grant dead.

He'd thought about how he'd make this knowledge pay off for him. He'd paid attention. Donnie had figured the smile on his face didn't make any noise as he'd relished thinking about what *he'd* do.

"We're going to pin it on the new guys. Tanner, Wilkins and Clark. We'll make sure they're near and throw them in, put the weapons in their hands and split. With a knock on the head, they'll be so out of it they won't know what to do. So many witnesses will say they did it, it won't matter that they deny it. Bloody hands, ya know?"

Donnie had almost gasped at hearing his name. He hadn't, though. He'd stood, like a stone statue, long after the others had left the latrine. Then planning came in, and he'd managed to get to the top. He convinced the right people he had information he would be happy to trade for early release. It had been a hard sell, but he was talking about the lives of three of their best guards and the take down of some of the worst instigators inside.

He'd gotten his release, but it was handled in a very quiet manner. This was a situation where the prison system didn't want to admit they were releasing a felon early without the usual procedures, but they'd done it. He had to follow the protocol by meeting with the parole officer and agreeing to the counselling, yada yada, shit. He was out.

The process didn't take as long as he'd thought. When he'd walked out, he'd become another person. He had papers that listed him as William McDonald. He'd insisted it be close to his own name.

Something else that was working in Donnie's favour? No one would recognise him. The last six months of his incarceration had been spent changing his appearance. He'd lost weight and gained muscle. Having spent a lot of time outdoors, he'd turned brown and his hair was gone. Just the mention of the word lice had him getting it shaved while inside and keeping it that way. There were several tattoos on his body now, some visible, some not. He'd practiced enduring pain and had gotten better at it.

Now he was ready.

A different man. His different look and new name made it possible for him to move around without anyone recognising him. It wasn't as if there were friends and family happily awaiting his return. They'd never know what hit 'em.

Donnie hadn't decided whether he was going to kill Jamie and Grant together or one at a time so the other would suffer. That's what he was leaning towards. And that damn dog. He was definitely going down. But that was long in the future. He was going to play first. They were going to go crazy trying to figure out what was going on. Because he had learned patience. It's the little things that drive you crazy. He'd figured that out the hard way. Now he was going to use it.

Chapter Three

Grant watched as Jamie shook the water from his hair, reminding him of Brit. They'd both finished their duties in the 'Hunk' booth and were in the back curtained off area changing into dry clothes. Jamie's short, blond hair didn't take a lot of drying or care, but Grant's was getting long, and it was only Jamie's begging that kept Grant from cutting it. Grant had started pulling it back into a tail with a band. He'd feel silly if it wasn't for the way it felt with Jamie's hands in it. It was worth the ribbing at work to see the lust in Jamie's eyes and feel those fingers playing in it.

"Well, that was fun. Coolest I've been all day. Let's get some junk food and walk around. We could try the little midway thing they have with the booths. Want me to win you a teddy bear?" Jamie teased.

"Goof."

"Yours."

"Yeah, mine," Grant answered in their usual banter.

For the next couple of hours, they acted like the kids they were supporting, playing games, joking around, laughing and enjoying life and love in the summer night.

They'd both won several stuffed animals and given them all away to girls who squealed in delight at the gifts. They were laughing as they sauntered to Grant's truck in the parking lot of the big high school where the carnival was being held. Grant almost walked into Jamie as he stopped abruptly.

"Hey, what's...shit!" Grant stepped around Jamie and saw what had stopped him in his tracks. The side of Grant's beautiful truck was scratched down the length, from front to back. Not just once, but three times. Most of the time, when a vehicle was keyed like this, it was just a swipe down the side. This had taken someone some time and effort.

"Damn, Grant. I'm sorry, man. That sucks." Jamie went to it and bent to look closely.

Grant joined him to see how deep the gouges were. Some of it wasn't bad and could be sanded out and repainted, but there were a few places that were deep. He didn't know about fixing those. It was just an object, true, but Grant loved his truck. It was always clean and shining and taken care of diligently. He turned to look at Jamie, his heart in his eyes.

"There's not anyone to turn in. How do we even report it? This could have been done any time in the last four or five hours. Should I call the police or is this too trivial for them?" Grant asked, looking to Jamie for guidance while he was still in shock. Damn it.

"No, it's not trivial. It's vandalism, whoever did it. I say call them. It could be kids, but it looks malicious. You know who my first thought is?" Jamie asked, looking from the truck to Grant.

"Coach Gilbert?" Grant nodded his head in agreement.

He'd not heard anything from the coach, and the assistant had taken over as he'd figured. But, that didn't mean the man didn't have a hard-on for getting even with Grant.

"I'm calling it in, and I'll see if Officer Johnson is there. He turned out to be a good friend last year." Jamie took out his cell and made the call while a distraught Grant continued to survey the damage.

"Oh man, Mr. Stevens, is that your truck? Dude, that's seriously whacked!" This comment came from a high schooler who was passing by with a couple of others. They all had girls with them. The whole group stopped to look at the scrapes down Grant's truck and shake their heads. High school boys understood truck-love. Grant recognised a couple of them, including the one who was looking intently at the scratches.

"Any idea who did it?" asked Eric, who'd bent to look more closely. "You know what? My brother's car got keyed a while back and this doesn't look the same. Look here, see how right here…and down here, you can see like a double groove? It looks like someone used something like a Phillips-head screwdriver and just drug it across, so it made a double line in some places. Not that that information helps any, but I just noticed it."

"Thanks, Eric. I hadn't caught that. I'll show it to the police when they get here. If we had a suspect, the police could check out keys and tools and look for paint residue." Grant laughed at himself a little, and added, "Too much CSI, huh?"

"No, Grant, it makes sense," Jamie said, closing his phone and heading over to where they were gathered. "It would be easy to check out. It wouldn't take much to see if there were little paint particles left in the grooves. Here's another idea, along the amateur detective line. Would you take your weapon home with you, or would you ditch it and run?" Jamie posed the question with a raise of his brows.

"Good question, Sherlock. But it would have your fingerprints on it, so wouldn't you take it with you?" Grant threw back at him.

"Maybe he wore gloves. That would make it seem a lot more premeditated," Jamie said, his mind obviously racing.

"Well, I doubt if it was a spur of the moment keying…or screwing, as the case may be," Grant said then grinned ruefully as the young ones all laughed at his turn of phrase.

He took it well and even came back with, "Go ahead and laugh. It's not your baby that's been…uh, screwed." More laughter followed, and Jamie nodded in approval.

"You're taking this awfully well. I'd be furious," Eric said.

"Oh, make no mistake. I am furious. If I could get my hands on who did this, I'd…" he paused, not being able to say such ugly things in front of the young people.

"I know. You'd throw them out of the park," one girl said, shyly, peeking up through her bangs at him.

"Good one. Yeah, I'd do that all right. More like, press charges and make him pay to have it fixed."

"You don't think it might have been, you know, the coach you threw out the other night, do you? He was pretty mad," said the girl, trying to be helpful, he was sure.

"I don't know, hon. We've called the police, and I guess they're on their way. Thank you all for stopping and hey, man, thanks for noticing the difference in the scratches. I'll pass the info along." Grant was glad for the information but didn't want them there when the police came, especially if it was Officer Johnson. He wanted to be able to talk freely with the lawman.

In a few minutes, the group sauntered on, and before long, a patrol car appeared. Grant sighed in relief as Officer Johnson stepped out, shaking his head.

"Who'd you all piss off now?" he asked, walking over to them and shaking both their hands. "Hey guys, how have you all been?"

"Up until tonight, great, sir. No problems. We came out from the carnival and found this." Grant pointed to the scratches and told the officer what the young man, Eric, had shown him. They all made a careful study of the difference in the scratches all down the truck and the officer concurred.

"I've seen a lot of cases of vehicles being keyed, usually anonymous vandalism, but this was more intense. This wasn't just someone walking by and flipping the finger, so to speak, at someone's shiny new truck," Officer Johnson said, tilting his head. He was quiet for a moment, thinking. He looked around the lot and pulled his head back up when his eyes lit on a big trash dumpster, not far from where they were.

"I'm following you, sir. Jamie already wondered if he might have thrown whatever he used away before he left," Grant said.

"You all stay right here, I'm going to just check it out. I'll call you over if I need your help digging through the trash," he joked with them, but was all seriousness when he walked over to the bin.

Grant and Jamie stood together, leaning on the grille of the truck, watching as the officer raised the big, yellow lid and flipped it back. They watched him shake his head and wave them over.

As they got near, he said, "I guess it was too much to hope that it would be lying in here on a clean sheet of white paper with little pieces of paint laying around. Looks like someone had too much to eat at the fair," the officer said, waving his hand in front of his face. Jamie and Grant leant over and jerked their heads back at the smell. Indeed, someone had thrown up right into the trash.

Grant moved down a little and looked closely at the litter in the big dumpster. He turned, and a tiny flash of silver caught his eye. It wasn't in the trash, though. It was on the back wall of the bin.

"Hey, you all look here," he pointed.

"Don't touch anything," Officer Johnson warned, unnecessarily, as Grant had no intention of touching anything in that mess. But that was silver paint.

"Well, I'll be damned. Looks like paint to me. I bet he opened this up and threw it in, hitting the back and sliding down. What do you think? Reckon it's down in there? All I can say is I'm glad I'm not looking in the other end," the officer said.

Grant was impressed when he saw the man reach into a pocket and pull out a pair of gloves, snapping them on as he hopped a little, placing his waist on the rim of the dumpster and leaning way over into it, so he could reach down the back side. Jamie and Grant were both presented a nice view of the man's behind as he bent over his task.

Grant laughed when Officer Johnson brought his head up and turned to look back at them and said, "Stop checking out my ass."

Jamie cracked up, too, and raised his hands in the air, joking, "Can't help it. It's a nice one. But I'm totally satisfied with the one I've got."

"Jamie!" Grant said, not really shocked, but a little embarrassed in front of the officer.

"Grant! It's the truth. Relax. The man is cool with it."

"Aha! What's that word you use when you've found what you're looking for?" the officer said, his voice a little distorted from being nearly upside down and having his air breathing constricted for so long.

"Eureka?" Jamie asked.

"That's it. Look what I found," the officer puffed as he gave a heave and jumped back down, making sure he didn't scrape the front of his body on the rim and didn't hit the orange-handled screwdriver in his hand. He held it at the base of the silver rod—in case there were fingerprints, Grant figured.

"Let me bag this and get a pad from the car. Grant, can you let the tailgate down and we'll sit for a while and you can give me your statement. I'll write up what I found, too. It'll save you a trip to the station. Nothing else we can do here." Johnson headed for the patrol car and they headed for the back of the truck.

* * * *

"Hey." Jamie said, into the quiet of the bedroom.

"Yeah?" Grant answered. He snuggled into Jamie's side, loving the tired, sated, happy feeling he experienced nightly before he slid into sleep. When they'd first begun their relationship, Jamie had jokingly listed all the special rules and benefits to a gay relationship. They both enjoyed the cuddle after sex rule, but one of Grant's biggest joys was going to sleep with as much of his body touching Jamie's as possible. He'd never dreamed how much the gift of touch would mean to him.

"Do you really think that coach is the one who scratched your truck? He did give you a really dirty look before he took off. You think he might be dangerous?" Jamie had obviously been lying there thinking about what happened earlier and the possibility of more aggressive acts.

"I don't know, Jamie. I don't really know him that well. I've umpired a couple of his games before and he's never been what you'd call sportsmanlike, but last week was really out there. Between the two of us, we attract the crazies, don't we?"

"God, don't even go there. Just promise me you'll watch out for yourself. Kind of be aware of things. Maybe this is a one-time thing, but you know I couldn't live without you."

"Right back at ya, Jamie. You're my life now. I enjoy my job and the people I've gotten to know, but you, you rock my world. Every day, I love you more. I'll be careful."

"I love you, too, Grant. Now, let's sleep. I'm fading fast and you've got to be tired, too."

Grant yawned, proving Jamie right, and soon, they were cuddled up close together, arms and legs entwined.

The next morning, Grant was up first. He let Brit out and stood, stunned, as once again Brit flew off the patio and went straight to the same spot he'd gone to the night he'd freaked out. Brit just growled low in his throat, pawed at the fence then looked back at Grant. Grant wondered again what was going on. He slipped on a pair of sandals and headed out to Brit.

Grant walked up and down, checking the fence to see if something could have gotten in through a loose board. He found nothing. He focused on the area that seemed to be freaking out Brit but found nothing there. The fence was well made and while it wasn't set into the ground, there was only about an inch below it.

Grant looked all around the backyard, feeling pride in the way it looked. He had helped Jamie with the plans they'd talked about last year. They'd bought a good-sized crepe myrtle and placed it in the back left corner. It was just starting to show beautiful dark red blooms. It would be full of them soon. There was a row of flowers down the left side of the fence. A vegetable garden, small, but productive, was in front of the flower garden, closer to the house for convenience.

Brit was focused on an area that was under the tree limb that came over the fence from their neighbour's yard. It was a large limb, and they had decided that it looked healthy and would cause no damage to their property so didn't make a big deal of its being there. They'd even talked about putting a couple of chairs back there under the ample shade provided by the huge limb.

He and Jamie knew the young couple who lived in the house behind the fence. Casey and Marsha Fine were nice and seemed to be accepting of Jamie and Grant's relationship. They'd even invited them over for a couple of meals. They were out of the country right now for a couple of month's vacation in Europe. They'd told Grant and Jamie how they'd both saved up vacation time, even foregoing a honeymoon, in order to get that much time away. Another of their neighbours was watching the house for them.

"Come on, boy. Let's go in. Do your business, and I'll get your food for you. Jamie's sleeping in." Brit took one more moment to look threateningly at the fence then walked around the perimeter of the yard while Grant headed back in.

"Hey, morning, love," Grant said, as he came in to find Jamie standing at the counter. Grant moved over to take a kiss, snuggling into Jamie's open arms. They stood, nuzzling and nibbling, greeting the morning in their preferred manner. They stepped apart only when they heard Brit at the back door.

Jamie went to let him in, and Grant got the dog's food ready with a fresh bowl of water. Turning to the fridge, he pulled out bacon and eggs, butter and jam. Putting his goods on the counter, he reached for a skillet to begin making breakfast.

"Will you make the coffee and pour us some juice?" Grant asked, turning to find Jamie watching him. "What?"

"Nothing, just thinking how lucky I am. You want straight coffee or flavoured this morning?" Jamie asked, moving to get the items Grant had asked for.

"Straight, I think. Did you see Brit freaking out at the fence again a while ago?"

"No, what happened?" Jamie paused, looking from Brit to Grant.

"Not much. He just went to that same spot and growled. I went out and checked it, but saw nothing wrong. It's weird. He must smell something there, some animal maybe." Bacon sizzled as Grant moved around, breaking eggs, putting toast in and setting the table with Jamie. In between checking on the meat and stirring the eggs, he made many opportunities for brushing against a willing Jamie.

"You keep on and your delicious smelling breakfast is going to get cold," Jamie warned, caressing Grant's backside as he turned back to flip the bacon. Grant just gave a little shimmy and cast a flirtatious look over his shoulder.

"Patience. It's Sunday. I plan on going right back to bed after we clean up from breakfast, and you get the paper in." Grant laughed when Jamie headed right for the front of the house to grab the paper and lock the door again. Jamie's eagerness did Grant's heart good. He loved, loved, *loved* that man.

As they finished breakfast, the phone rang. Grant got up and handed it to Jamie while he started to clear the table. He stopped when he heard Jamie say, "Yes, sir, he's right here. Let me pass it over to him." Jamie passed Grant the phone, and they traded places. Jamie started on the dishes while Grant listened as Officer Johnson greeted him.

"We're fine, sir. Do you have information for us?" Grant looked up at Jamie, who stood still, plates in hand, waiting to hear.

"I hate to tell you this, but there were no prints on the screwdriver. I'm going to check around and see if that coach you mentioned has an alibi for yesterday and last night. I just wanted you to know I'm not going to ignore this. It looks like more than just random vandalism."

"Thank you, sir. I appreciate it. I'll take the truck in tomorrow during my lunch hour. I'll see what the dealer thinks about what can be done about the scratches. Thanks again." Grant hung up after the Officer said something and just looked at Jamie, shrugging his shoulders.

"Nothing to be done. He's going to see where Coach Gilbert was yesterday. Let's just forget it, and head back to bed with the paper and some more coffee."

Jamie looked like he wanted to say more, but he shrugged and continued to the sink with the dishes. In no time, working together, they were back in the bedroom, sharing the paper and sweet, coffee kisses. Before long, the paper was on the floor and they were entwined again.

"I love lazy days. Kiss me lots more. I'll never get enough of your mouth," Jamie said, reaching for Grant. Never having been one accused of being slow, Grant opened and accepted Jamie's invasion, moaning. The sheer joy of being able to move his naked body against Jamie's and indulge in the intense feeling of being complete when they were together made Grant grateful every day for his life with Jamie.

"More. I want you." Grant was suddenly frantic for a deeper connection.

"You've got me, Grant. I'm all yours," Jamie assured him, leaning up and putting Grant onto his back, coming up over him.

"No, I mean I want you inside me. Right now, Jamie."

Jamie raised his brows for a second but didn't hesitate in meeting Grant's desire. Leaning over his lover, Jamie reached into the drawer by the bed and got what he needed. He handed the condom to Grant with a husky, "Get me ready." He proceeded to do the same for Grant, using the lube to moisten and stretch him.

Grant drew his knees up and met Jamie's eyes as Jamie pushed into him. "Ah, yes, Jamie. Just like that. Come here, please, come down here," Grant begged, reaching up for Jamie. He loved it when Jamie took him like this, face to face, so he could see his lover's gorgeous blue eyes blazing with his feelings. Those full lips were drawn tight over his teeth as he thrust all the way into Grant. He did lean down as requested, though.

Putting both hands up, Grant cupped Jamie's face, drawing it to his own. He sucked on Jamie's bottom lip, slid his tongue into Jamie's mouth and began his own thrusting motion. Jamie's breathing was hard against his cheek as Grant kept it up, tangling his tongue with Jamie's and sweeping in and out. One of his hands slid to the back of Jamie's head to hold it still for his plundering tongue. He was amazed and impressed with Jamie's ability to continue thrusting into him while actively involved in the kisses.

"God, Grant, can't breathe. You take my breath, make me crazy. I'm not going to last much longer." With those words, Jamie pulled back and reached to grasp Grant's cock in his hand. Gliding and sliding, twisting and pulling, Jamie had Grant ready to shoot in a very small amount of time.

"Now, Grant. Come on," Jamie encouraged, squeezing and rubbing his thumb over the tip of Grant's cock. That was it, all it took. Grant came with several hard jets of cum, covering Jamie's hand and pooling on his own abdomen. Jamie straightened and took hold of Grant's legs, pushing into him one, two, three more times before Jamie, too, came hard, filling the condom and nearly collapsing onto Grant. He managed to ease out and discard the condom before he toppled onto the bed, half on and half off Grant's welcoming body.

"God, we're good," Grant said.

"Mmm-hmm," Jamie mumbled, against his shoulder, before turning to open his arms for Grant to slide into. Grant plastered himself to Jamie and was soon taking a nap against Jamie's chest.

Chapter Four

When Grant told Jamie how much it was going to cost to take care of the mess on his truck, Jamie was suitably aghast. A little over a thousand dollars, for scratches! He tried to explain to Jamie what the man at the dealership had told him about buffing and having to feather the deep gouges and then fill in over and over until the gouged places were no longer evident. Then primer and paint on the whole side of the truck.

"I'm seeing many hours of overtime in my future. I'll have to take every chance that comes along. Don't think 'asshole screwing my truck' is covered on the insurance policy." Grant couldn't keep the disgust out of his voice.

"I'm so sorry, man. That really sucks. I'll help on it if you'll let me."

"No way, Jamie. My problem, especially if it was Gilbert. On to other topics, please." Grant was tired of this one.

"You're not working Sunday afternoon, are you? I'm scheduled to take Brit to the centre then I thought we'd go see Miss Wilhemina. I was hoping you'd come with me for both," Jamie said.

"Sure. I love taking him there. I know how much he helps the patients, having been on the receiving end myself. Count me in." Grant remembered how torn up he'd been about the death of his dog in the accident that sent him to the centre last year. Jamie bringing Brit in had helped bring Grant out of the depression he'd been experiencing because of his situation.

Grant had grown up in the foster system and was pretty much a loner in his personal life. He'd been coaching at a high school in Crandall, a town about two hundred miles from here when the accident happened. On spring break, he'd been travelling alone when a drunk driver had crossed over the median and made Grant's the middle car in a twisted metal sandwich.

At the time, Jamie had been a tech at the rehab centre. Jamie'd had to spend a lot of time helping Grant because they were both big men and Grant could do so very little for himself due to his massive injuries. Grant had been attracted to Jamie from the first, but having never addressed the fact that he might be gay, he'd been hesitant about many things. But Jamie was impossible to resist.

"That's great. I enjoy going more when you're with me. I'll call and make sure Miss Wilhemina is up for a visit. We also need to have her over again for a cookout soon," Jamie said, making notes on a pad at the kitchen table.

Jamie loved all the little old ladies he worked with, as a physical therapist now, having finished his studies. His LOLs, as he called them, benefitted greatly from Jamie's compassion and caring. But Miss Wilhemina, he loved in a special way. She was ninety-nine now, and Jamie knew she'd be gone soon, so he kept in touch with her as much as he could. She had no one left, and Grant loved watching Jamie with her.

"Okay, it's a date for Sunday afternoon. About two again?" Grant asked Jamie, as that was when they usually went. "How about after we bring Brit back from seeing Miss Wilhemina we go out for supper?"

"You're right, Handsome. It's a date." Jamie teased Grant, using Miss Wilhemina's name for Grant.

"Smarty. I've got to go now. I have three games to cover tonight. I'll be in late," Grant said, standing to put his early-supper dishes away. He'd worked his schedule to where he could have a meal with Jamie before he went in to work tonight. "What are you going to do all night?"

"I could come watch you," Jamie said, standing also and clearing the table.

"You don't have to watch all my games, Jamie. You're not trying to watch over me, are you? I'll be fine," Grant swore, bumping shoulders with Jamie at the sink.

"I know. I'll quit hovering. Maybe I'll go online and check on decks. I'm really excited about screening in the patio then extending it and having a deck behind it. We can still have the grill on one side, and the idea of a hot tub on the other side of it is a great one. I'm so glad you brought it up. I'm going to do some research and see about how we could swing it. I also love the idea of a fire pit out back. It'll be fun building it together." Jamie put his hands on Grant's shoulders and turned him towards the bedroom.

"Go get ready. I'll finish here. If you need me, call. Otherwise, I'll have information for you when you come back. I'll also call our buddy and tell her we're coming to see her Sunday."

"You're not sending me off without a kiss, are you?" Grant paused to ask.

"You're not gone yet, are you? When have I ever sent you off without a kiss?"

Grant admitted, "You've got a point there."

* * * *

Grant had to admit he was uncomfortable every time he saw the administrator of the rehab centre. Bob Wilkins was a good man, but he was Donnie's father. That just gave Grant the creeps. Jamie still worked for the man, and he could handle it, so Grant felt like he should man up and try to get over his awkwardness around the man. Just because his son had tried to kill him in order to get to Jamie, had done one cruel thing after another to hurt Jamie. Yeah, so maybe he still had a problem, but he worked on it for Jamie.

Grant stood with Brit while Jamie talked a few minutes with Bob. He could tell that Brit was anxious to get to work. Grant actually thought that Brit loved coming to visit the patients. Being very calm and loving, Brit was perfect for the job he did here. Grant was tickled when Brit whined, getting Jamie's attention and causing him to finish his conversation and join them.

"Come on, let's go share the love. You ready, Brit?" Jamie asked, reaching out a hand for Brit to shake. Brit woofed softly and shook hands.

Later, after Brit had been to several of the rooms and been rubbed, patted, scratched, hugged, and loved over and over, they headed to Miss Wilhemina's . Grant had fallen nearly as hard for the old lady as Jamie had. She was a marvel to him. At ninety-nine, she was very young at heart. Jamie had told Grant that she didn't have anyone special in her life anymore, having outlived family and friends. She loved Jamie and Grant and adored Brit.

They got bad news when they got there, though. Miss Wilhemina wasn't feeling good. This was new to them. Most of the time, she was up and eager to see them. The lady in reception told them that Miss Wilhemina wanted to see them, but the woman suggested they keep it short. In other words, don't disappoint her, but don't tire her further.

"Maybe you should just go see her without Brit and me," Grant suggested.

"No, I don't think so. She'll be more upset if we don't all show. We'll know if we should leave. We might just go in and give her a kiss and tell her we love her, let her pat Brit and take off. Whatever she wants," Jamie insisted.

Brit seemed to know something was different. He padded quietly down the hall with them and stood at the door when they reached her room. Grant still held back and let Jamie go in. At first, he thought the little old lady was asleep, but when she realised Jamie was there, she opened her eyes and smiled.

"Jamie, sweet boy, there you are. Where's my other handsome boy? Oh, there you are," she said, after seeing Grant hovering in the doorway with Brit. "Come on in here now. I'm not dying, I just feel a little under the weather. Don't you worry. I can see it on your faces."

Grant and Brit headed over, and Brit put his head on the blankets by her hand. She immediately smiled and smoothed the top of his head. She reached for the bed remote and raised the head of it so she could talk to them more easily.

"I'm so happy to see you all." She was trying valiantly, but she seemed so tired and worn down.

Grant was really worried about her. He knew it would hit Jamie hard when she passed on. He watched as Jamie bent to kiss her cheek and smooth her hair. One of the things that had drawn Grant to Jamie in the first place was his huge capacity for caring for others. He really cared very much for the clients he worked with, but this sweet lady had stolen his heart and had drawn in Grant as well when he'd shown up in Jamie's life.

"Well, Handsome, aren't you going to say hello to me?"

Grant went to her and bussed her cheek, too. Jamie went around to the other side of her bed and sat on the side of it, motioning for Grant to do the same on his side.

"How long have you felt bad like this?" Jamie asked, taking her other hand in his. He moved his thumb gently back and forth across the back of the wrinkled, spotted hand. Grant knew that touch was important to people who were confined like she was.

"Hey, Miss Wilhemina. I'm sorry you don't feel well," Grant slipped in when she didn't answer Jamie immediately.

"I'm fine. The doctor has seen me, and I'll be better soon. He gave me some medicine and said I'd feel fine in a couple of days. Stop worrying, now, and tell me what you've been up to lately."

They talked for a few minutes and soon Jamie got up. Grant had noticed she was about to fall asleep. She patted Brit and told him he was her special puppy. Grant took Brit and let Jamie tell her goodbye. He heard Jamie tell her that they'd check on her and invite for a cookout again when she was better.

Jamie joined him in the hall and he noted how worried his lover looked.

"You think she'll be okay?" Jamie asked him.

"I hope so. She's a tough one. I'm hoping it's not her time yet." He brought his hand up to touch Jamie's back. The power of touch again. Jamie leaned into him a little, accepting the gesture for what it was.

"Yeah, she's stronger than most people ten or fifteen years younger. I'm going to miss her, Grant, when she's gone. I know she won't have much longer."

"She loves you, Jamie. You've made her life happier, and that should really count for something," Grant told him as they got into Jamie's car, his truck being in the shop.

"She's enriched my life, too. She's something else."

Jamie was quiet on the way home, and Grant knew he was thinking about the lady they'd left. Grant reached across and took Jamie's hand in his and brought it up to his mouth for a quick kiss. Jamie kept his eyes on the road, but he smiled and dropped that hand to Grant's thigh, squeezing gently.

They pulled up and as soon as they got out of the car, Brit started whining. He ran up to the door and barked. Grant looked at Jamie and they both shrugged. Hurrying up to the door, opening it and going in, they stood, stunned, as Brit literally jumped into the house, barking and growling, viciously. He didn't sound as if he thought there might be a rabbit in there and he was interested. He sounded as if he wanted to kill something.

Grant and Jamie rushed in and literally couldn't keep up with a totally freaked out Brit. He ran from one room to the other, growling low in his throat as if he were warning someone. He was at the back door then back to their bedroom. They caught up with him there. He was in the closet and he was turning in circles and looking in corners and rooting around like he was following a scent. He barked and came over to them then went back and barked again. Grant and Jamie were both looking closely at everything to see if the house had been broken into, but nothing seemed out of place.

"What the hell, Jamie? He was like this at the back fence the other morning. Just barking and growling like he could smell or see something, but I couldn't find anything. No sign of an animal, nothing wrong with the fence, nothing period. He just freaked. Is there something wrong with him?" Grant would hate that for Jamie.

"Man, I don't know. I don't smell anything that he could be after. I don't see where anyone has been here. I don't understand. Brit! Hey, come here, boy. What's up?" Jamie tried to get his pet to come to him, but Brit just looked at him the same way he'd paused and looked at Grant the other morning at the fence. Turning away from them, he ran to the kitchen and barked and growled at the back door.

"Watch this," Grant said, as they followed, "I bet he goes to the same place at the fence. See if you can figure out what he sees." Grant opened the back door and again, as predicted, Brit hurled himself from the patio, through the yard, and nearly ran right into the fence in the same place he had before. Brit seemed to be crazy, snarling and growling as if he wanted to kill something. He looked back at them and paused a second, as if to see what they would do. When they just stood there, watching, he turned back and pawed at the fence, growling.

"Let's go see. I don't think we'll find anything this time either, but he's sure mad about something. I'm beginning to wonder if he's okay," Grant said, stepping off the patio and heading to where Brit wasn't calming down a bit. He barked and whined, growled and snarled. Grant and

Jamie walked up and down the fence, looking closely for any sign that there'd been any kind of animal there.

They found no evidence of any visits from the animal world, and again there was nothing wrong with the fence. They checked it very carefully. It was wooden and there weren't spaces in between the vertical slats at all. It was solid and tall. They couldn't even see their friend's house. They could see trees in their yard, but nothing seemed to be moving in them, like a cat or something that might have sent Brit into a frenzy.

"Brit! What's wrong, boy? Come here, now. Brit! Here, now!" Jamie slapped the side of his leg and Brit stopped abruptly. He stood a moment and looked at the fence, barked once, then turned and walked over to Jamie, almost reluctantly.

Grant was really getting worried about Brit. This was twice he'd seen Brit act like this with no obvious reason. Could he be sick, maybe something like a brain tumour or something? He almost laughed at himself for thinking such out there ideas. Less than an hour before Brit had been just fine, sweet and docile for Miss Wilhemina. But wasn't that just what made it so weird? One minute totally fine, the next he was like a wild thing.

God, don't let there be something wrong with Jamie's dog. It had almost killed Jamie last year when that idiot, Donnie Wilkins, had poisoned Brit. Jamie's beloved dog had nearly died, and Jamie'd been horribly distraught. Grant had been there for Jamie, and thankfully, Brit had come through.

Grant watched as Jamie knelt on the grass and moved his hands over Brit, who stood still, accepting the exploration. Jamie crooned to the dog, moving his hand over and around, patting and rubbing. Brit licked Jamie's face and whined. Brit pushed and Jamie went over, laughing. Grant watched as they roughhoused a few minutes, smiling indulgently at them.

Brit stopped and looked up at him and barked, this time an obvious invitation to join the fun. Grant wasn't stupid. He bent and rubbed Brit's head, but Jamie grabbed him and pulled him down with them. Grant laughed and crawled over to straddle Jamie, who immediately grabbed his hands. Hmm, maybe to keep Grant from tickling him? Jamie laughed with him as they wrestled a bit on the ground. Brit barked happily now, playing with them, leaning in to lick Grant's cheek this time.

"Ew! At least, we match now." Grant pulled one hand free to rub on Brit, looking at him closely and seeing nothing different about him. He shook his head, deciding to put it off as just strange animal behaviour.

"What are you thinking about?" Jamie asked him.

"I was just deciding to put Brit's behaviour down to strange animal stuff. He seems fine now. Besides, I have better things to do, sexy things, love you things." Grant said, leaning down to put his hands on the ground beside Jamie's head, and covered his lover's mouth. Brit licked a big swipe from Jamie's ear, up his cheek, onto Grant's cheek and on to his ear. That brought Grant up in a hurry.

"Brit, yuck! Go on now." Grant laughed and scolded at the same time, rubbing his hand across his wet cheek. Jamie was doing the same thing.

Jamie took hold of Grant's shoulders and held on while he sat up. Now they were sitting up, facing each other, on the lush green grass.

"We can finish this here, or we can go inside, wash our faces, and finish it in the bed...with the door closed."

Jamie said, holding Brit off with one hand and holding Grant with the other.

"I vote for the inside location." Grant moved his hips against Jamie's and they both groaned at the contact.

"Up, up. Let's go," Jamie insisted, pushing Grant, clearly eager to get the show on the road or, at least, in the house.

They got up, laughing and pushing each other, reaching down to play with Brit, too. Inside they trooped, giving Brit some fresh water and a treat then heading for their room. Brit tried to follow, but they closed the door on him. Grant must have looked a little guilty, because Jamie laughed and pulled him towards the bathroom.

"He's fine. He's got the whole rest of the house. Come on, let's get the dog slobber off our faces then see about making love. Want to cook out later?" Jamie asked him, as he ran water in the sink.

"Sure, later. Right now, here, let me," Grant said, taking a washcloth from a basket on the sink that had several rolled up in it. He wet it, added some soap and moved it over Jamie's face, all over, saving the doggy side for last. Rinsing the rag, he smoothed it over Jamie again, cleaning off the soap. Very quickly, Grant did the same to himself and turned to Jamie, who'd watched him silently the whole time, his eyes at half mast, looking sexy as hell.

Grant leant over and ran his tongue up the same cheek Brit had earlier and laughed at Jamie's gasp.

"Is that better?"

"Oh, yeah, do it again," Jamie said.

Grant was about to follow orders when Jamie turned his head and caught Grant's tongue in his mouth, sucking it in. Grant leaned further into him and swept right through Jamie's mouth. Jamie met his tongue, and they played tag and tangled and teased until both were breathing heavily and pressed together tightly. Jamie began pulling Grant shirt from his jeans and up his back. Grant reciprocated and they stepped apart simultaneously to tug both shirts over their heads, mouths meeting again as soon as they were clear.

"Mmm," Grant mumbled, and Jamie replied with, "Mmm-hmm."

Grant eased away and began to remove his jeans, watching as Jamie mirrored his actions. Soon, they were pressed against each other again, much more happily now. Grant lined his chest and his hips up with Jamie's and moved against his lover in ways he knew would have Jamie moaning soon. They were both so tall, with Grant just a bit taller than Jamie, but his torso was longer, so their hips met perfectly. They knew this, because they'd practiced this many times.

Rubbing their cocks together like this had them both eager to recline and take it further. Grant moved his hips, causing his cock to slide up and down beside Jamie's, both of them hard and leaking a bit. Jamie bit Grant's lip, eliciting a gasp, then his tongue came out and soothed the tiny hurt. Grant now went after Jamie's tongue, bringing it into his mouth and sucking on it, rhythmically. Jamie thrust his hips against Grant's.

Grant reached into the drawer of the cabinet by the sink without even looking and grabbed lube and condoms and started walking, pushing Jamie backward into the bedroom. Jamie grinned and turned to grab the cover on the bed and flip it back. He swivelled back just in time to get his arms full of Grant who bore him down to the bed.

"Hello there, Handsome," Jamie whispered.

"Every time we come home from seeing her, you call me that. You're the pretty one in this pair, and you know it,"

Grant told him. Jamie's blond hair and blue eyes made him quite the gorgeous hunk. Grant loved him more than he could say, and the beauty had little to do with it. Jamie earned his love every day in many ways.

"You've got an interesting look on your face again. What's up, baby?" Jamie asked him.

"Thinking about how pretty you are...and how that's not the reason I love you so much," Grant admitted.

Jamie blushed nicely for him, and Grant bent to nuzzle against his red cheeks.

"You're my one and only, too. And Miss Wilhemina has it right. There's nothing wrong with her eyesight, you know. You are handsome with your black hair and blue eyes. Can I take your hair down?" Jamie asked.

"Yes, you know you're the only reason it's not short. I know you love it, and I love your hands in it." Grant turned his head, giving Jamie better access to the back of his head. In seconds, his long silky hair slid over his shoulders and down to brush either side of Jamie's face. As he expected, Jamie's hands came up to caress both the hair and Grant's head. Grant shivered as he felt Jamie's fingers massaging and scratching his scalp then sliding down the length of his hair. Watching as Jamie took the ends and rubbed them over his cheek and down his neck, made Grant want to do other things, wicked things, with it. Then he figured, why not?

He planted a kiss on Jamie's mouth and started moving backwards. Grant took his time, planting kisses and using his hair to caress Jamie's chest and stomach on his way to his goal. It was easy to tell when Jamie realised what he was going to do. Jamie sucked in a deep breath and held it.

"Grant? Oh, God, that feels...mmm, heavenly," Jamie said, gasping.

Grant moved so the tips of his hair brushed over Jamie's sensitive cock. He moved his head back and forth letting the length of his hair sweep across Jamie's hips, lying in the creases between his legs, dragging on Jamie's balls and lying finally on his hips and thighs as Grant settled between his legs.

Both of Jamie's hands were now on Grant's head as Grant bent eagerly to his task. Taking Jamie's cock into his mouth, he moved down on it, as far as he could reach. When he felt it nudge the back of his throat, he swallowed, tilted his head, and took it just a bit farther. Jamie groaned and his fingers clutched in Grant's hair, not hurting, but egging him on. Not needing the encouragement to do what he loved, Grant continued until Jamie came hard in his mouth, noises that were almost words coming from over Grant's head.

"God, Grant, you melted me completely. I love you, man," Jamie finally managed to get out, reaching down to pull Grant up to him.

Keeping hold of Grant, Jamie used the motion to bring him up and turn him so that Jamie leant over Grant. Grant looked up at Jamie and smiled, thrilled that he'd made Jamie happy and excited with the look on Jamie's face now. It boded well for Grant's immediate future. Jamie bent to kiss him, and Grant opened eagerly to the questing tongue, giving himself up to the feelings that Jamie drew from him, had always drawn from him.

Grant had learned a lot from Jamie in the time they'd been together. Coming to this relationship a total virgin, Grant had been an empty canvas for Jamie to cover with images and touches that filled his life and his heart with joy. There was nothing that Jamie had ever done to or with him that Grant hadn't enjoyed. Jamie had been so good to him, teaching him and letting him explore on his own. The journey had been one that they had both enjoyed tremendously, and Grant felt that now they knew each other very well. Grant knew how to turn Jamie on with a touch or a look and Jamie knew the same about Grant.

Hell, they both loved full-out fucking, in most any position, but it was the other forms of lovemaking that they liked to find variations in. Jamie loved Grant's blowjobs and Grant loved making Jamie happy. He'd become quite the master. If his hands weren't busy now, moving over Jamie's back, he'd pat himself on his. Grant went wild when Jamie sucked on his balls while he fingered Grant's hole, and Grant knew from the look on Jamie's face that he was about to be one happy lover.

"Grab your legs and let me at you, baby. Come on, your turn to be a puddle of well-loved man."

Obeying Jamie's directions, Grant reached down and grabbed behind his knees, pulling them towards his chest. It amazed him that he could be so comfortable with someone that he could assume such a wide open vulnerable position. Jamie never made him feel awkward, though. He manoeuvred himself into the space between Grant's legs and slid his hand down the backs of Grant's thighs, to his upturned cheeks. All the while, he looked down at Grant's eyes.

"I love you, Jamie," Grant said, voice husky with emotion and the tightness of being bent double. He saw Jamie's eyes glow with the words and had to bite his lips to keep from yelling when Jamie bent his head to lick his balls and take them one at a time into his mouth to roll and tease and suck, gently at first, then harder. One of

Jamie's hands went to Grant's cock that bobbed and leaked. The other went down to tease Grant's hole that clenched against his tiny invasion. Grant rested his legs on Jamie's ample shoulders, leaving his hands free to touch Jamie's head, caress his hair.

Grant reached over to the table by the bed for some lube. He passed it down to Jamie and soon a slick finger inched its way into Grant. He bucked once then settled into the intense ripples of pleasure that spread from his hips to other parts of his body in a sensual tide. The tips of his fingers tingled as he tried to grasp the cover and hold on as Jamie loved him. Jamie moved his lips from Grant's balls to the base of his cock, licking and sucking, moving from there to the sensitive area behind Grant's ball sac. Grant panted and moaned as Jamie worked him over, moving his finger in and out and adding another before going for Grant's prostate.

"Jamie! Please, again. God, I love you. I love how you touch me, how you know me. Please don't stop." Grant gave up talking for breathing then and rode the storm until he could take it no longer. He shot long ribbons of cum onto his stomach as Jamie kept all those varied movements going until Grant finally came down from the high he'd reached.

This time it was Jamie who crawled up, reached over to the table for the now, ever-present hand towel they kept there. He cleaned Grant's stomach and dropped the cloth over the side of the bed.

"Come here, hold me," Grant said, raising his arms up for Jamie to settle onto him. He loved to feel Jamie's full weight. For the first bit of their time together, they'd had to be careful of Grant's recovering body. His whole right side had been bent broken, scraped and torn, and it was a while before he could take Jamie's body full out on top of his. But, he'd come to love the feeling of being held down with the wonderful pressure of Jamie's body, settling onto him. It made him feel so…taken, so loved.

Jamie knew how much Grant loved the feeling, so he settled on top of Grant and they lay, both catching their breath, kissing, nuzzling, sighing, basically coming down. Grant smoothed his hands over Jamie's back, applying pressure up and down Jamie's spine, relaxing his lover even more. Their cookout might be a little late getting started, he thought, as Jamie's eyes closed and he sprawled.

Grant rolled and Jamie was on his side, without really waking. They moved a little to get comfortable, and in just a few minutes, they were napping and slept hard for about an hour.

Neither of them was aware of the shadow on the window. Brit was, though. They both jerked awake when their bedroom door burst open, and Brit was across the room and nearly through the window.

"Jesus! Brit, what the hell? What is it?" Jamie was up and at the window, drawing the blinds up. He looked out but saw nothing. He even unlocked and opened the window, leaning his head out to see if he saw someone or something. Nothing. But Brit wasn't giving up. He still barked and growled and put his paws up on the sill. He snarled and whined, looking at Grant and Jamie then going back out. They heard him in the kitchen, barking and growling at the back door.

"Not again," Grant said, up and reaching for shorts for both of them. They went to the door and let Brit out and, as expected, he was off like a bullet, headed for the fence, the same place as before.

"What do you think's going on? Is he really after something? Is something going on? Or is there maybe something wrong with him? He's never like this. Only when Donnie was at his worst, but he's in prison, so this doesn't make sense." Grant put his hand on Jamie's arm and stroked, knowing Jamie had to be worried, too.

Jamie stepped off the porch and went around the side of the house to their bedroom window. Grant followed him and watched as he looked at the grass. They couldn't tell if there was anything disturbed. It was grass, short grass, at that, having been mowed lately so there were no prints of either animal or person. It was a puzzle.

"He's calming down back there. I say we start the grill, make some supper and eat out here. Maybe if we spend some time out here with him, he'll calm down more. I'm stumped, Grant. I can't imagine what's up with him. I don't even know how he got into the bedroom a while ago. It wasn't locked, but it was latched. It's too weird. Come on, steak or chicken tonight?"

"Chicken with your barbeque sauce on it, please. I'll do the salad and some corn on the cob. I'll make some fruit tea, too. Just for you," he said, reaching to take Jamie into his arms for a hug.

Grant promised himself that if Brit went crazy like that one more time, he would insist that Jamie take him to the vet for a check-up.

* * * *

It was all Donnie, AKA William, could do to keep from laughing aloud as he listened to them wigging out over the stupid dog's behaviour. He was loving it. The dog's craziness was an added bonus. It was driving them mad, and that was his ultimate goal. Well, not the final goal, that was their death, but this was too much fun.

Donnie sauntered into the house right behind theirs that he'd broken into and was using. He never turned on a light. He didn't have to, the couple who were gone on vacation had them on timers to come on at certain times, so he just made sure he stayed away from the windows. He knew from snooping that they would be gone for about six more weeks. There were no plants so no one would be coming in to mess with the place. There was no mail stacking up, so they must have had the post office keep it for them. All good things for him.

Donnie did begrudge his targets their supper as he opened a can of Vienna sausages and ate them with crackers. That barbequed chicken had smelled good. Damn it.

Chapter Five

Just as Grant had geared himself up to try and talk Jamie into taking Brit to the vet for his weird behaviour, it stopped. For a couple of days, all seemed normal. Work was hot and tiring but interesting and enjoyable, too. Jamie was doing well with his new physical therapy work and found it rewarding and Grant knew from Jamie's comments that he still went around and saw his LOL's every once in a while.

They had checked back with Miss Wilhemina and she was doing much better and sounded great. She wanted to know when they were cooking out, so they invited her for the upcoming Saturday afternoon.

Grant was a little late going in since he planned on being really late coming home tonight, with three games to umpire after the regular workday. He wasn't sure if Jamie was coming to watch or not. He remembered their shower together that morning, and they just hadn't gotten around to plans for later.

After cleaning up the kitchen and putting a pot roast into the crock pot with potatoes, carrots, and onions,

Grant set the cooker on low then went to check on securing the house before he left. Jamie would be happy to have the meal waiting for him when he got home Grant knew he'd grab some when he came in, tired and hungry himself.

He sat now at the kitchen table and wrote a note for Jamie. One of the things he'd loved when they were first together was finding the notes that Jamie would leave for him all over the house. When he'd read the first one, signed, *Love, Jamie,* his heart had turned over in his chest. Lord knew, he did love Jamie. So now, Grant did the same thing for Jamie, often leaving him notes and of course, signing them, *Love, Grant.*

This should be perfect at about five-thirty. Enjoy the meal. I'll have some when I get home. I'm excited about the new deck plans. Sorry I can't join you and Brandon with Brit at the centre today. You are my sunshine. Love, Grant.

He taped the note to the window in the back door so Jamie would see it as he came in, since Grant knew that he preferred coming in that way. They seldom used the front door. Grant remembered seeing a plaque that said "Backdoor guests are best." Maybe they should get one put up. Their friends had even started knocking on the back door instead of the front. He wondered just for a second if it might have something to do with the fact that one of the things that Donnie Wilkins had done to them last year was paint on their door *Motherfuckin' faggots live here* in red paint. He'd marvelled at the fact that Donnie had known to put the apostrophe since he'd dropped the g. In a 'Fuck You' gesture, they'd painted the door red the next day.

Grant gathered his equipment and uniform for later that night and headed out, locking the door, checking to make sure it was secure. Knowing all was well, and he'd left his lover a nice meal for later, made him feel good. Doing things for Jamie made him feel like a true partner. As he headed off the side steps of the patio, he glanced back. He was looking forward to helping with the new deck. They had such a large backyard, the new addition would work in easily and be a lot of fun.

* * * *

Jamie grinned when he saw the note taped to the back door. He hurried in to take it down. He stopped right inside the door and sniffed. Wow, something smelled wonderful. Brit met him with a woof and he bent to give him a rub. He looked over at the counter then down at the note. Aw, his baby had left a meal cooking for him. His heart thumped, thinking of Grant taking the time this morning before he left for work. He read the note and moved to put it in the drawer with the others they were collecting. Love notes. He couldn't resist taking the top off the cooker and sniffing deeper. One of his favourite meals.

Replacing the lid, he turned to Brit.

"Smells good in here, huh? Come on, let's get your gear and go to the centre. Brandon is meeting us there. This is a quick one today, just on my lunch time. We'll be back here in about an hour or so. Let's go, boy." Jamie gathered Brit's vest and leash and off they went, locking the back door. Brit stopped and looked back towards the fence, gave one warning growl and a bark then turned back to Jamie. Jamie shook his head and they left. What was going on with his dog?

A little over an hour later, they were back and again Jamie gave an appreciative sniff when he opened the door to the wonderful smell of meat and vegetables cooking.

Brit started barking as soon as they got in the door. He ran around the kitchen table, growling and barking, nose to the floor, sniffing.

"Brit, what in the hell has gotten into you? Are you okay? What is it, boy?" Jamie looked around but didn't find anything different. He walked through the house but found nothing amiss. Brit had never left the kitchen, and he still growled low in his throat.

Jamie sat down in a chair and called Brit over to him. Brit came immediately, and he looked closely at his dog. He seemed to be okay, eyes clear, mouth clean and everything the right colour. Jamie felt all over his head and found no odd bumps or knots. He rubbed all over Brit, looking for bites or other spots that might mean he'd been bitten by something that would cause him to go a little freaky. He found nothing odd.

"What is it with you, huh? You've been freaking out a lot lately. You've got me a little worried. Everything okay now? Huh?" Jamie bent and kissed the top of Brit's head and stood up. He watched as Brit went around the table one more time, but he seemed to be settling down.

After making sure that Brit had what he needed, headed back to work. Tonight, he planned to go to one of the home supply stores and look around for things they would need for the deck. He might go on over to watch Grant finish up, too. That never failed to entertain him.

* * * *

Grant was hot and tired by the end of the second game, and he still had one to go. He grabbed a bottle of water and swigged half of it down. He heard someone call Jamie's name and turned to see his love standing at the concession counter. He hadn't thought Jamie was coming tonight. He started to walk over and watched as Jamie bought a hot dog and a drink. He hadn't thought Jamie would be hungry after the supper he'd left for him. He snuck up behind Jamie and said, "Still hungry?"

Jamie turned and smiled at Grant.

"Hey. Uh, there was a problem with the cooker. When I went in to get Brit I know it was on and smelled like heaven. Thank you for doing that, by the way. But when I got home this afternoon, ready for a super meal, though a lonely one, it was off. None of it was done, the veggies were hard and the meat wasn't cooked. I had to throw it all out."

"Aw, man. I'm sorry," Grant said.

"It wasn't even warm any more. I guess the electricity went off or something after I left. I hate that, too, 'cause I was looking forward to it. Maybe the cooker is just broken, some kind of malfunction thing. We can check it when we get home. Sucks, though."

"Yeah, big time. Well, I tried to surprise you," Grant said, spreading his hands in a wide gesture.

"Oh, you still get the points and the reward even if it didn't get done. The thought was there, and that's what counts. I'll see you later. Have a good game. I see they're getting ready to start." Jamie bumped shoulders with Grant and headed up to the top of the bleachers while Grant turned back to the field. Damn. He'd been looking forward to a snack later, too.

He called the game and met Jamie afterwards in the parking lot. He had his truck back now and was almost afraid to bring it to the games. That had been one expensive vindictive gesture by someone.

He'd heard back from Officer Johnson, who'd told him that Coach Gilbert, according to his wife, had left for a fishing vacation. Johnson had said the wife had seemed glad that her husband had taken off, saying she hoped he stayed a long time. She'd said he'd left the day after Grant had thrown him out of the park. So did that mean he had an alibi, being gone at the time, or maybe he hadn't really left until after he'd vandalised Grant's truck in a payback gesture. Who knew?

"I'll see you at the house. You going straight home?" Grant asked Jamie.

"Yeah. I'm looking forward it. I'll make you a peanut butter and jelly sandwich then we'll clean up in the shower."

Grant laughed and said, "You're not dirty like I am."

"I will be right after we get home. You don't think I'm waiting 'til after you've cleaned up to kiss you, do ya? And if I kiss you, I'm gonna be all over you, so see, you'll be all over me, too. Hence the need for a joint shower. Makes perfect sense to me."

Grant laughed again and got in his truck, in a hurry now to get home. Jamie followed him and pulled in right behind him in the driveway. They heard Brit barking as soon as they got out of their vehicles. Both ran towards the back door. Grant was in the front, and he couldn't have said later why he reached for the doorknob without putting the key in first. But he was surprised when it turned, and he went right in. Jamie had forgotten to lock the door. Brit came over, pushed past him and headed straight for the back fence.

Jamie was there, looking from Grant to Brit in the backyard, barking and growling.

"What the hell?" Jamie asked.

"Did you forget to lock the door? It wasn't locked," Grant asked.

"No, I didn't forget. I never forget. You don't either. I was careful because Brit was going cuckoo again, around and around the table, sniffing and growling. I sat down with him and checked him all over for bug bites or anything that might make him act like this. Man, something weird is going on. You sure the coach guy is out of town?"

"According to his wife, he is. He must not be a model husband either since she seemed relieved that he was gone. You think he's got something to do with this?" Grant wondered. Did the coach even know where he lived?

"Well, there's nothing to report. Nothing seems to have been done. Let's look around inside and see if anything is missing. Hell, that doesn't make sense. Nobody is coming in here with Brit here. He wanted outside! There's nothing in here now. Grant, I know I locked that door."

"I'm sure you did. Come on, love. Let's go back there and see if we find anything this time. I'm worried about your dog, Jamie. This isn't like Brit. You think it's safe to take him to the centre with him freaking out all the time?" Grant hated to bring it up, but what if he went off with a patient?

"I don't think he would, man. It's only here that he ever freaks out. Inside and at the fence. Something is fucked up, big time."

They went to the back fence, looked around and tried to calm Brit. It didn't take as long this time. Grant stood by Jamie, looking at Brit. He reached out and put his arm around Jamie, knowing that Jamie had to be worried about Brit's odd behaviour.

"Do you think it's time to take him to Doc Kevin? They can run some tests and see if there's something wrong. I hate to say it, but it just seems like such bizarre behaviour, Jamie. We can't ignore it. What if it's something that can be fixed? Maybe he did ingest something or get bitten by something." Grant moved his hand on Jamie's side, caressing him, supporting him. He wasn't about to bring up the brain tumour idea he'd had earlier.

"Yeah, I'll call Kevin tomorrow and see what he thinks I should do. I'm glad you're here with me. I couldn't handle it if something was really wrong with him...and I didn't have you." Jamie dropped to his knees and slapped his thigh.

Brit stopped his growling and looked at Jamie. It was as if he could tell that Jamie was really stressed and hurting. He immediately came over to Jamie and put his head on Jamie's shoulder. Jamie's arms came around Brit's neck and they hugged for a few moments. Grant told himself he wasn't a wimp for getting misty-eyed. Ah, to hell with it. He knew how much these two beings loved each other. Brit could tell something was bothering Jamie and he was there to comfort him. By the same token, Jamie knew something was wrong with Brit, and he would do what he had to in order to help him.

"Come on now, you all are tearing me up. Let's go in and have a snack, clean up, and just sit in front of the TV for a little while, even if we have to watch Food Network. We just need to snuggle and relax.

"Okay, sounds like a plan. You ready to go in, boy? Come on, Brit," Jamie said, getting up and heading back to the house. He reached out to Grant and Grant took his hand, squeezing hard.

Grant made sure they did just as he'd suggested. They gave Brit a treat and some fresh water. Jamie and Grant rifled through the cupboards looking for something to tide them over without having to cook. Grant looked at the clean cooker in the sink and asked Jamie if they should try it again or throw it away.

"I'd say throw it out. If it is messed up, we'll just have to chuck another expensive meal. It would probably be cheaper to just get another one. I'll put it in a bag and put in the trash now. You finish eating then it's shower time, followed closely by snuggling on the couch. TV is optional."

Grant said, "I like the way you think."

On his way to get a trash bag for the slow cooker, Jamie bent down and kissed the side of Grant's neck, saying, "I like the way you do everything."

"Good to know." Grant started to say something about hoping everything was going to be okay with Brit, but he didn't want to make Jamie think about that right now.

Grant headed for the shower and was already in when Jamie joined him. Once they were both wet, he turned and took Jamie into his arms, wrapping his around Jamie's neck and holding on. Jamie put his arms around Grant, one high on his back, one low. They held each other for a while in the stream of cool water, providing love and support and the healing power of touch. At first, that's all it was, but of course, in a little while, it became more.

They shifted as cocks rose and rubbed together. Jamie put his lips to Grant's neck, and Grant tilted his head, giving him better access. He loved it when Jamie kissed his neck and right below his ears. Jamie knew it, too, going right there first. Grant shivered and held Jamie tighter. Grant had learned that Jamie loved to have his nipples sucked. He moved back just a bit and bent to do just that.

It could have been awkward, but Jamie moved back a little to give Grant room and Grant thrust his hips forward to meet Jamie's. Grant felt as if they performed like in a dance, shifting and turning to allow one or the other to reach their goals. Groans filled the shower stall as they pleased each other. Their hips pressed together, just enough to slide their cocks against each other, causing shivers and goose bumps to rise on both bodies.

Jamie took the band out of Grant's hair and moved his hand in it, letting the water course through the sweaty strands. That felt so good to Grant, he took one hand and slid it down Jamie's torso, ending up with a handful of hard cock. Making the most of a perfect opportunity, he began to jack him off, slowly at first. He reached for the liquid soap and used it for lube and was back in seconds, jerking harder and getting great approval sounds from Jamie. It wasn't long before Jamie came on his hand. They turned and the wash of water cleaned it all away and down the drain.

Jamie now turned again and eased Grant against the wall. Grant jerked as his back hit the cool tiles.

"Warm the water a little, that's cold. I'll shrivel up, and you won't have anything to grab onto," he teased Jamie.

"Yeah, right. This long thing isn't likely to go anywhere," Jamie retorted, but he did turn the hot up a little before coming back to Grant. He moved right into Grant and used both hands to cradle Grant's cock. Jamie put his face in Grant's neck and started talking to him as he moved his hands in a counter rhythm, twisting, turning, sliding along the length of Grant's cock, making him moan.

Grant didn't know if it was the touching or the talking that turned him on more. He had to admit that he loved it when Jamie did this in that low sultry voice. He thought he'd shoot in record time. The closeness, the intimacy of the shower, the words pouring over him, and the hands that created magic all worked together to increase the sensuality of the moment.

"You know how much I love to make you come, don't you? You're the only man I've ever loved, Grant. I'm going to be loving on you when you're old and grey and can't get it up anymore. I'll still caress and hold you and make love to you in new ways. I'll kiss you all over and tell you how good you make me feel and how special you are. Like now, you take such good care of me. Oh, you like that? You can't seem to be still, can you? You're about to come for me. Come on, lover, you know you're almost there. Come for me."

And just like that, Grant did. His hands had been flat against the shower wall, trying to hold himself up, but now they wound around Jamie again, and he held on while he tried to get his breath back.

"I love you so much," Grant said, barely able to speak.

"I know, baby. I love you just as much. Come on, let's wash up and get out of here. I want to just hold you for a while."

"Yeah."

* * * *

It being Saturday, Jamie was surprised when Grant said he would go with him to see the vet with Brit.

"Don't you have to work today?" Jamie asked.

"I should, and I may yet get called in, but I told them I had something important to do today. We have the cookout this afternoon with Miss Wilhemina, so I'll be here to help get that ready, or to go pick her up if you'd like. I want to go with you to see Doc Kevin." Grant wanted to be there for Jamie if the news was bad.

"You don't want me to be alone if the news is not good. I know you. And you say I'm *your* sunshine. Come here, baby."

Grant came over for the kiss Jamie was offering.

"Have I ever told you how much I love it when you call me baby? I'm such a big, tall thing, it doesn't make sense, but it warms my heart anyway, coming from you." Grant meant it. If anyone had told him over a year ago that he would be in a gay relationship and be happy to be called dear and baby and sweetheart, he'd have sworn they were crazy. Now he craved it. Being Jamie's baby was a wonderful thing.

"I'm glad. You are my baby, and you're my big manly man lover, and the other half of my existence. I'm glad you're going with me. Kevin said he'd fit us in at about ten-thirty. How about after that we go shop for this afternoon, get something sweet for Miss Wilhemina? She loves her sweets. Cake, pie or brownies."

"She loves brownies. I guess chocolate is a woman thing no matter how old they are," Grant said.

"Hey! Watch it. I've been called a chocoholic myself, you know? I think brownies would be perfect. Bought or made here?"

"Oh, made here. Maybe she and I can do that while you man the grill. She'll love being able to help. I'll do most of it. She can sit and order me around."

"Mmm, I've got some orders for you later tonight," Jamie said, suggestively.

"Oh, you do?"

"Mmm-hmm. You'll like them. Come on, let's go get this over with," Jamie said, turning to Brit.

"Come on, boy. Let's go see Doc Kevin. Yeah, that's a good boy," he said, as Brit went to the door and waited. He liked visiting the vet, unlike most dogs who ran when it was mentioned.

They went in Grant's new truck, the backseat perfect for Brit. Kevin was ready for them when they got there and luckily they didn't have to wait. Being worked in, Grant had figured they'd have to wait for an opening. It took a few minutes for them to explain all the incidents where Brit had acted like, well a mad dog. All the time they were talking, Kevin had Brit up on the table, running his hands over the dog, checking his mouth, his eyes and his ears. Grant figured he was looking for ticks, bites, bumps, or tender spots. Nothing seemed to be wrong. When he was finished, he looked at them, puzzled.

"There's nothing evident for sure. He seems to be in fine shape. I'll take some blood samples and check for anything in his system. If that doesn't turn up anything, I'd suggest taking him to Lexington to a specialist for a CT Scan. That would give us a more accurate reading if something was really wrong. Don't worry yet, Jamie. Let's get the blood tests back first," Kevin said, patting Jamie's shoulder. Jamie looked as if he were standing, frozen, in front of a train.

"Come on, let's don't borrow trouble, Jamie." Grant put his arm around Jamie's shoulders and hugged. "Today's hard part is over, soon as Doc is finished. We'll go play now. Get food, get our little pal, and enjoy just being together on this pretty summer day."

Just like clockwork, as soon as they arrived home with the groceries, Brit couldn't wait to get out of the truck, barking already. He jumped out and cut across the backyard like a wild thing. He growled and barked then ran back to the back door and stood growling.

Grant and Jamie looked at each other, grabbed their cloth grocery bags and hurried to the door. Jamie was in front and went to put the key in, but the door swung open as soon as he touched it. Not again.

"Grant, didn't you lock this when we left?" Jamie asked, turning to look back at him.

"Of course, I did. I always lock it then check to make sure it's locked. I got into the habit back when you-know-who was around. I swear I did, Jamie."

"Hey, it's okay. I believe you. Remember the other day. It was on me then, and I know I locked it. Something is just weird, Grant." Brit had pushed past them and was inside the house, doing his crazy-dog thing. He was going from room to room, barking and growling, sniffing and snarling. It was getting a little creepy.

Grant followed Jamie in. They sat the bags on the counter and went to help search the house, looking for any clue to Brit's behaviour. Nothing. Jamie finally got him calmed down then they put the groceries away and took him into the backyard for some play time. He ran around and wrestled with them, going after his ball over and over, and seemed fine. On occasion, he would glance over at the fence where the shade from the big tree limb was and stop in his tracks, but then he'd almost shake himself and return to the game.

Grant and Jamie went in and took a quick shower, with minimal hanky-panky. There were some kisses and holding going on, of course. It was too good a chance to pass up. Being closed up and wet together was a perfect lead in to passionate kisses and tender embraces. They didn't even jerk off. Grant felt sure that Jamie's mind was on his dog and their plans for the afternoon. He was present for the caresses, but a little distracted. Grant understood.

It was decided that Jamie would take Brit and go pick up Miss Wilhemina in Grant's truck, while Grant got the ingredients ready for the brownies. He marinated the chicken and wrapped some potatoes in foil to put on the grill. It wasn't too far to the facility where she lived so Grant soon heard them return. He hoped Brit didn't lose it again and scare Miss Wilhemina.

Chapter Six

Miss Wilhemina had loved her ride in the new truck. She came in the back door glowing and going on about it.

"Grant, what a lovely truck." *Lovely?*

"Why thank you, Miss Wilhemina. I like it," Grant answered. *Lovely?*

"Oh, I felt so grand sitting high up there. It's a good thing for Jamie, though, or I'd still be in it. Lord, I'd have to have a kid's sliding board to get out of the thing. And I swear I never saw so many knobs and dials and such on the dash. It certainly isn't anything like our old truck we had on the farm. It was such fun, Grant."

"I'm glad you enjoyed it, Miss Wilhemina. I've always wanted a truck, and after the accident, I just decided to go for what I wanted. I got lucky on that one, too."

Grant and Miss Wilhemina had a grand time in the kitchen. He had tried to make her stay seated and let him do most of the work, but she was up and down like a jack-in-the-box. At one point, she asked where the measuring spoons were and he said they were in a drawer by the refrigerator. Before he could get them for her, she was up and had opened the wrong drawer. Uh-oh. That was the drawer that he and Jamie had been storing their notes to each other.

"Oh, what's this?" she teased him, picking one up. She glanced at it and dropped it quickly, turning a bright red. She stepped back suddenly and almost overturned. Grant caught her and eased her over to the table to sit.

"I'm sorry, hon. Those are just little love notes that Jamie and I leave for each other. I'm sorry if it embarrassed you," Grant said. Thinking about it, he wondered why she was so embarrassed, though. He went to close the drawer and his eyes fell on the note she'd dropped back in. He gasped.

"Shit! I mean, sorry. Jamie!" Grant called, holding the note in his hand.

He could hear Jamie's feet pounding across the patio then Jamie stood inside the kitchen door, looking from Grant to Miss Wilhemina and back to Grant.

"What? What's the matter? You scared me to death."

Grant handed him the note.

Grant, I'm going to fuck your ass 'til you scream! Love, Jamie.

It was Jamie's turn to gasp, followed by the same curse and the same apology as Grant's.

"Grant, I didn't write this. I swear it. I never..." Jamie stood, looking stunned, holding the offending note in his hand.

"Miss Wilhemina found it in the drawer, uh...looking for measuring spoons. We're so sorry, ma'am, we really are. That's not the kind of notes we write. Look," Grant said, reaching into the drawer and pulling out a few more, "please, read a few."

Jamie, I'm looking forward to some quiet time with you tonight. Love, Grant.

Grant, I loved falling asleep on the couch with you last night. My life is richer with you in it. Love, Jamie.

Grant, thanks for helping out at the centre with me today. Brit and I both think you're wonderful. Love, Jamie.

Jamie, there's a surprise in the refrigerator for you. Love, Grant.

"You see, we never write anything like that. We don't even talk like that for the most part. I'm so sorry you had to read that," Grant said.

"Did you show her the one where you said I was your sunshine?" Jamie teased him, but with a loving smile.

"Stop, goof," Grant said, wondering if Jamie would finish it like they always did. He should have known.

"Yours."

"Yeah, mine. My goof."

"Oh, shush. Relax, boys. You don't think I don't know *how* you make love, do you? I have to admit, I was a little shocked at the wording, but I believe you. I don't think the men who write these sweet things would write that. So, who did?"

"I don't know. This is the weirdest thing yet. As if there wasn't enough going on," Grant said, not thinking.

"Why? What's going on? Come on, boys, tell me. Is someone bothering you again, somebody like that Donnie last year?"

"We weren't going to tell you about it. We don't want you to worry," Jamie said, reaching over to pat her hand.

"Tell me everything over supper. You all are not in danger again, are you? I mean, Donnie is safely put away in prison, you said, so...well, wait until we sit down to supper. Then, you all are going to spill the beans, you hear me?"

"Yes, ma'am," Grant and Jamie answered together.

Through supper, the three talked and thought aloud and planned and tried to figure what was going on.

"Jamie, do you think maybe someone is coming in your house when you all are gone? Only when you are gone with Brit? That would explain why he goes crazy when you return from somewhere. He smells someone. You all don't. Am I right that this is the first *thing* you've found? It's always just been his odd behaviour?" Miss Wilhemina was a smart old bird.

"You're right. We didn't see that. I guess we're too close to it. It just didn't click with us that it's only...no, wait. Jamie, remember the other night just as we were falling asleep, Brit came flying in and almost went through the window. What if someone was out there then and he could smell them? That would make sense. And the time we came home and he was barking inside the house. That was the first time the door was unlocked. I bet someone was going to come in, heard him inside and left. Someone has been coming in our house, Jamie!" Grant knew he sounded agitated, but the thought freaked him out.

That night, outside their window. Could someone see in? Did someone watch them making love or listen to them? That really set off his *ew* metre. He made a mental note to go outside the window and see if he could see in when the shades were down. He remembered they had been that night. They weren't always because they had the privacy fence so no one could see in. But if someone was *inside* the fence...

"The fence!" Grant said, suddenly, jerking his head around to Jamie.

"Of course, the fence. That's why Brit goes so crazy at that one place on the fence. But we've checked it over and over and it's solid, no board loose, nothing out of place, no sign of any animals," Jamie said, tilting his head in what Grant called his thinking pose.

"I'm calling Officer Johnson and running some of this by him, but not tonight. This explains a lot, and it took Miss Wilhemina to figure it out. Thanks, sweetie," Jamie said, leaning to kiss her cheek. She blushed, this time not as bright.

"I smell brownies. Let's have hot brownies and ice cream to finish off the meal. Soon we'll have to take you back. We can't tell you how much we appreciate your helping us with this," Grant said, getting up to ready the dessert. He knew Jamie was putting off calling the policeman because he didn't want Miss Wilhemina any more involved. Hell, Donnie had nearly killed her last year. Grant figured they'd take her back then plan the next step.

"You just make sure you keep me informed. Don't leave me wondering if something has happened to you all over here."

"We will, I promise," Jamie said, clearing the table so Grant could put the chocolaty treat down for them.

"Oh, that smells heavenly. Let me tell you a secret. You never get too old for chocolate." The expression on her ninety-nine year old face rivalled that of a toddler at a birthday party. Anticipation had her eyes shining and her smile glowing.

"We're so glad you came today, Miss Wilhemina. We enjoy your company so much. I'm sorry it ended up on a sour note, no pun intended," Jamie said.

"Dear boy, it ended on a sweet note, pun intended. I think it's delightful that you all leave little notes like that for each other. It's the little things like those, and small things you do for each other that make a relationship special and lasting. Don't let this stop you from leaving little surprises for each other. You all will get this figured out."

"We will, and we'll keep in touch," Jamie promised her.

"I have something I want to ask you boys to do." She seemed a little hesitant.

Jamie went right to her side and knelt by her chair, taking her hand.

"Anything for you. What is it?"

Grant stood just behind Jamie. She looked at Jamie then Grant and blushed. Grant wondered what in the world she would say.

"All my life, I've been Wilhemina, even as a child. The only person who ever called me anything else was my husband, and he's been gone for almost twenty years. I would like it if you all would call me...Willie. It's special to me, and I would only allow it from someone I, well, someone I loved. Would you all do that for me?"

Grant hoped the moisture in his eyes didn't turn into big drops of girly tears. God, she was a sweet thing.

"Of course, we will. I know I feel special even being granted the privilege, Willie. It feels weird, though. You sure you wouldn't prefer Miss Willie?" Grant asked.

"Look at you, you are so proper. I've never known more sweet, kind and mannerly men than you two. I know I call you my boys, but I know you are men. Calling me Willie makes it seem more like we're just good friends. Do you mind? Will you be uncomfortable?" She looked from one to the other again.

Jamie leant over and kissed her cheek. Grant went around and kissed the other one.

"I'm proud to call you friend, Willie. The 'Miss' was just out of respect. If you prefer to be just Willie, then it would only be respectful to grant your wish. Willie it is," Grant promised her.

"Come down here, you giant thing you." She motioned for Grant to kneel by her side like Jamie was.

"I'm only going to say this once. I won't embarrass you all again. But I love you both so much. You have made my life so much richer. I can't believe you even want to spend time with an old lady like me, but I'm not stupid, either. I'm grateful. I have no one left, family or friends. You're it for me. Don't think I'll forget that when the time comes." With that weird statement, she held her arms out and Jamie and Grant both leaned in for hugs.

Here was this tiny lady with her arms around two big men, kneeling beside her. It must have looked like they were worshipping at her feet. They damned near were, come to think of it.

"Now, I think it's time for you to take me back. Then you all can call your policeman friend and get started on this without worrying about me," she said, proving she'd known all along what their plans were.

Again, Jamie and Brit took her back while Grant stayed behind and cleaned up the kitchen. He was humming as he wiped down the counter when the phone rang. Spreading out the rag and putting it on the edge of the sink to dry, he reached for the kitchen phone.

"Hello."

Nothing. Not even breathing. That was weird. He hung up. As soon as he did, it rang again.

"Hello," Grant said then after a silent pause, "is anyone there?"

The phone clicked. Someone had been there. A chill went down his back. Someone was playing with them. He sat down at the kitchen table and took a deep breath. What to do? Make a list. He was up and moving to the guest room/storage room. He knew there was a notebook in here and some pens. Grabbing the things he needed, he returned to the kitchen.

When he heard Jamie and Brit at the back door, he realised there was no barking or growling this time. He made a note of that, too. With him here, nothing had happened that set Brit off.

"I'm betting you those blood tests come back clean and you can forget that trip for the CT Scan," Grant said, as Jamie walked in. "With me here, all is well on the home front. I bet, too, if I'd gone with you all, the story might be different. Can we call Officer Johnson now? Is it too late?"

"No, I don't think so. What's that you've got?" Jamie asked, sitting beside Grant, reaching over to cup the back of Grant's head and pull him in for a quick kiss. Grant decided quick wasn't what he wanted so he leant back in for more. He saw the smile as Jamie covered his mouth again, this time with more intent. Putting down pen down, Grant reached up to hold Jamie's face as their tongues shared the taste of chocolate and the need for comfort.

The comfort was so welcome that Grant got up from his chair and moved over, sitting right in Jamie's lap. Jamie was quick to wrap his arms around Grant but looked at him with his head tilted. Okay, not a regular happening, the lap thing, but Grant wanted to be in his arms right now.

"I'm freaked, Jamie. I can't help it. This is just a little too much like last year when Donnie was terrorising us. Someone called while you were gone. Twice. Hung up both times. No words, no breathing, but I heard them hang up." Grant didn't mind that he sounded scared. He *was* scared.

As he'd sat there at the table, making a list of everything that had happened so far that had seemed odd or out of place, it had added up, chillingly. All the times Brit had gone crazy, the scratches on his truck, the door being unlocked twice, the note, the calls, the window, the fence. It all made Grant's heart pound as he thought of something happening to Jamie.

Sitting as he was, on Jamie's lap, his head was way above Jamie's but he wrapped his arms around Jamie's neck and pulled Jamie's head to his chest. He kissed the top of Jamie's head. Jamie tilted it back, looking up at Grant.

"I love you. We'll figure this out together. It scares me, too. The thought of someone doing something to you chills me. Do you think it could be this coach? Should we find some way to see if he really went fishing like his wife said? That's the only person I know who would have a grudge against us?" Jamie tightened his arms around Grant.

"Against me, you mean. What if this is all my fault?" Another thought that chilled Grant through and through.

"Screw that. We're in this together. Anything that hurts you, hurts me, and…"

"That's just my point, Jamie. What if what I did causes someone to hurt you or Brit? I would just…I couldn't take that, Jamie. I love you so much," Grant put his forehead down to Jamie's and just closed his eyes. The fear and emotions were too intense right now.

"Hey. Enough. It's not you or me, it's us. Come on, let's look at this list and then we'll call Johnson. I hope he's on tonight. Hop up, baby, and let's take some offensive action. I don't like playing defence." Jamie popped Grant on the behind and then rubbed it better as Grant yelped.

Grant handed the list he'd been working on to Jamie, watching as he read down it. Jamie's eyes got big, and Grant asked, "What? What did you think of now?"

"The Crock Pot? The dinner you made me? What if, no, Grant, I know that goes on here, too. Brit was acting the same way, but he never left the kitchen when I brought him home from the centre that day. I didn't even look over at the cooker, because I'd sneaked a peek into it when I first got here. It still smelled great in here when we got back so I just assumed it was still on. I bet someone turned it off while we were gone. That's why he was going around and around the table. He could have even written the note then, too." Jamie's voice was getting louder and sounding madder the more he talked.

"That means he's going through our stuff. I mean, really looking through drawers and stuff. Remember that first night when Brit kept going back into the closet in our bedroom. This really stokes the creep factor big time." Grant shivered, thinking about somebody going through their personal belongings, their private life.

"Damn."

"What?" Grant asked, dreading more bad news.

"I wish we still had those cameras up from last year. I'm thinking that might be a good investment again. We'd have to be more careful about where we put them since

whoever this is must be coming in and out from the back."
That made Jamie pause and think a minute before going
on. "But how's he getting in? We've checked that fence
over and over."

"Not from the other side. It must be the tree. It would be
hard, though. It's so far up to that limb." Grant paused,
trying to picture someone using the limb to get over the
fence. It would be hard. "The Tuckers are gone. It
shouldn't be hard to go over there and into their backyard
and scope it out from that angle. We could see if there's
any evidence over there. Someone might not have been as
careful on that side, thinking we haven't figured anything
out yet."

"You know, this is all supposition. We may be way off
track here, but things are beginning to make sense, if we
follow this vein of thought. I think we're ready to call. You
add the cooker thing to your list, okay?"

Jamie called the police station and asked for Officer
Johnson. When told Johnson wasn't there, he asked for
Mark Thomas, another officer they knew from the
situation last year. Luckily, he was there. Officer Thomas
agreed to come over and take a report.

"That would be great," Grant heard Jamie say, "but we
were hoping to get Officer Johnson in on this, too. He
came for the first incident. I'd like having him on this
again."

"He's off today but was going to meet me when I got off
for coffee. I'll call him and see if he'll join me at your place.
He'll probably want to come over. It's a little out of the
norm, but not too bad. 'S workable. I'll be there in about
twenty, probably with your officer of choice."

"Hey, it's nothing against you..." Jamie started to say.

"Kidding, Mr. Taylor. Relax. Work on getting your facts together."

"Doing that. Thanks, sir." Jamie turned to Grant when he hung up the phone.

"Remember Officer Thomas, from last year? He's on tonight but says he can get Johnson to come over, too. I'd just feel better if he was here through this."

"I agree, Jamie. He was good to us, compassionate, helpful. We need to add those feelings to our chaotic ones right now. Let's look this over and see if there's anything we've forgotten, and if it's all in the right order." Grant took Jamie's hand and led him back to the table, but before sitting down, he wrapped Jamie in his arms and held on tight.

Jamie did the same, moving his hands over Grant's back in a soothing gesture. Grant put his face in Jamie's neck and sighed deeply. Why couldn't they just be allowed to work and love and be happy?

"Ever feel like you've got a big target on your back?" Jamie asked.

"Not funny, dude. I've got your back, you've got mine. We'll deal, okay?"

"Together, Grant. Always." Jamie moved his head and took Grant's mouth in a strong, passionate kiss of obvious intent. He was saying that there was nothing that could come between them, ever. Grant could feel that as if Jamie had spoken the words. They kissed for long moments, then just held each other. Eventually, they sat and went over the list they'd made, finding there was nothing they'd left out that they knew of, anyway.

Grant put on a pot of coffee and brought out the rest of the brownies as he heard car doors. The front doorbell rang, and Jamie went to let in the officers.

"Come on in. Grant has coffee and brownies in the kitchen. The list is in there, too. Thank you both for coming over without it being an emergency. We're really getting scared. Here, sit down, read this, first, if you will." Jamie went to help Grant get cups and plates for the brownies.

Grant watched out of the corner of his eye as he set the goodies on the table. Both officers read the list, more than once, making notes on their own tablets as they did. At one point, Thomas got up and went to the back door, opened it, knelt and took out a flashlight. For a few seconds he looked intently at the lock.

"By the way, I think it's time you all started calling me Wade," Officer Johnson said, sipping the coffee and reaching for another brownie. "I have a feeling we'll be even closer after this one is all said and done. I'm going to suggest right off the bat that you all do the camera thing again. It helped last year. We just might have to think about where you place them, make them a little less noticeable. What do you guys think?"

"Well, Wade," Grant said, smiling at using the officer's first name, "we already talked about it. We're getting ready to start adding on a deck back there. We're going to screen in the patio then put a deck behind it with the grill on one side and a hot tub on the other. We could sort of hide the actual placing of the camera along with us putting up the structure then it would be part of the overall mess of construction. Might be less obvious that way."

"Good idea, and I like the idea of the deck. You've certainly got enough room back there," Wade said.

"Wade, look at this, will you? Looks like someone might've scratched the door with something that left a thinner mark than a key would." Officer Johnson walked over, knelt down by Officer Thomas and looked closely at the mark in question.

"Could be. See, Jamie, Grant, it would be hard to tell if he'd used a pick 'cause it wouldn't leave a mark, being smaller than a key. But it looks like he might have either been in a hurry or careless, and there's a scratch here by the lock. Do either of you remember doing that with something thin?" Wade rose, as Jamie and Grant looked at the mark and shook their heads in tandem.

"No, sir. I don't remember missing the keyhole. You, Jamie?" Grant asked.

"Not really. So, who's surprised? I bet this happened when he tried to come in and found that Brit was here. He got the door open but had to leave in a hurry when fury came barrelling at him barking and growling. That's my Brit, come here, boy," Jamie said, reaching for Brit and rubbing him as he leant back on his heels.

Brit raised his nose to the door and growled low in his throat. For some reason, that made them all laugh.

"Case closed. He can still smell the bastard on the door," Mark Thomas said. They closed the door, settling around the table again.

"Is it too late to check it for prints?" Grant asked.

"Maybe not. I'm sure yours are all over it, but I can see if there are any others. We might get a clear one. I'll go get the kit from the car. Wade, don't eat all the brownies." Mark got up and went out to the car, and Wade looked at the list again as if puzzled by something.

"What's on your mind, Wade?" Grant asked.

"You threw away the slow cooker, right? Has the trash gone yet?" the officer asked, talking around a brownie.

"Uh, no. It goes out on Mondays. Do you need me to go get it?" Jamie asked.

"Yeah, but don't touch it. Do you remember if it was turned off or just not working? If it wasn't working, then you're right, it might just be a malfunction. But if it was turned off, then someone turned it off. If you didn't wash it, there might be a print there, too."

"I never thought of it. I don't think I turned it off. I just took the inside out of it and dumped it, washed it out and put it back in the base. I unplugged it and put it in the bag later. I didn't wash the outside off since I was going to toss it. I'll go get it," Jamie said, getting up and heading outside.

"Good thought. There's so much we've missed, thinking it was just coincidence or unrelated. Miss Wilhemina came up with the idea that it happened most when we had Brit out of the house," Grant told Wade.

"How is the old lady? Doing all right? God, she's got to be what, almost a hundred? And she comes over for cookouts and helps figure out crimes. She's a hoot."

"Yeah, we love her. Jamie already had a soft spot for her, and it nearly killed him last year when Donnie tried to smother her, just to hurt someone that Jamie loved. God, what an idiot. I think she has a birthday on November first. We have to do something big for her. She'll be the only hundred year old I know."

"Let me know. I'd like to come, too," Officer Johnson said, showing his compassion again.

"I can't believe we're being targeted again. And this time it looks like it's my fault. Jamie felt responsible last year. Now, I know how he must have felt. So, what's next?"

Right then Jamie came in with the trash bag that he'd used for the cooker. Luckily that was the only thing in it so he just passed it over to Wade. He must have heard Grant's question.

"Yeah, what's next? Will you check to make sure the coach is really on a fishing trip? Right now that's the only person we can think of who has a beef with us."

"Yeah, we'll do that. But tomorrow, I want to come back and go check out the other side of the fence and the tree that hangs over into your yard." Wade was cautiously opening the bag, and when it was open, he said, "Aha, see! It's turned off. You sure you didn't turn it off, Jamie?"

"I'm sure. I've been thinking about it. I didn't even look at the switch. I just unplugged it and put it in the bag with the clean inside pot in it. I set the lid on it with the cord inside and took it out. That's just more evidence, huh?" Jamie said.

"The fact that it's off is good info, and if there are prints, even better. It being tied up in this bag might make it easier to get a print. It may have helped set it with the heat and humidity."

"Ooh, sounds like CSI, huh, Grant?" Jamie said.

"Pretty much," Grant agreed.

"You all watch the Miami one or the New York one or the original?" Wade asked, grinning at them.

"Miami," Jamie and Grant answered together. Both stood and acted like they were moving suit jackets back out of the way before putting their hands on their hips and tilting their heads in the same gesture.

Wade laughed out loud and said, "Well, two Horatios, let's solve this one. Mark is almost done with the door. We'll take this with us. You all be careful and watch out for each other and Brit. Don't take chances. Get a deadbolt on that door tomorrow—and the front one. I'll get back to you as soon as I have any information. You call me if anything happens."

"Thank you, sir. We appreciate you taking the extra time for us."

"This isn't like a normal case, and I liked you two last year. I don't like to think of bad things happening to people that I've come to consider friends. I'm going to give you my cell number, another thing that's not often done, but if I'm not on, you give me a call if you need me."

"Thank you so much, Wade. This means a lot. Um, are you married, kids?" Grant asked.

"Not anymore. She decided she liked someone else better. Couple of years ago and I haven't even been looking since." Wade didn't sound too broken hearted.

"Maybe you'd like to come hang with us sometime when this is all figured out. We do cookouts with friends a lot. You'd be welcome," Jamie said, and Grant nodded.

"I'd like that. First, we catch this idiot. I'll get back to you. Oh, and thanks for the brownies. We don't usually get treats when we're on a case." Wade stood, items gathered and ready to go.

"As you said, nothing about this is normal. At least, Donnie is in for another four years." Jamie put his arm around Grant as they walked the officers to the front door.

Once it was closed, Jamie and Grant just looked at each other for a second before both of them opened their arms. Jamie pushed Grant up against the front door and reached for his mouth. Grant met it eagerly and opened for him. Grant put his arms up around Jamie's neck and held him close while they let the kiss take them away. Away from worry, away from fear, away from stress. Away to comfort, away to support, away to… passion. *Hello.*

"Mmm," Grant said, into Jamie's mouth, "I'm ready for bed. How about you? It's been a big day. The one good thing is that I don't think there's anything wrong with Brit anymore. I think he's a pretty smart dog. I was worried there for a while, and it hurt me to think you might lose him. I'd hate it, too, but you and Brit, man, you're a team."

"We're all a team now. Come on, I need you tonight. Quick shower then I want to forget everything except how much I love you and how sexy you are and how much I want you." Jamie pulled on Grant, heading for their room.

"Now that's a plan I can get," Grant reached down and slapped Jamie's butt and finished, "*behind*!"

Jamie turned and reached to do the same to Grant, saying, "Smart*ass*!"

Grant laughed at the absurd, juvenile jokes. They needed laughter now and love. He would see that Jamie got just what he needed. He chided himself for thinking even for a moment he was doing it for Jamie. He wanted Jamie just as much. He needed the love and the closeness and the passion, too.

They would use their bond, strengthened every time they made love, every time one did something for the other, every time they supported or encouraged each other, to meet and outmanoeuvre whoever was targeting them. If it was Coach Gilbert, they'd handle it together. Grant loved being an equal part of a team.

Chapter Seven

"You boys up yet?" It was Officer Johnson, uh, Wade, on the phone, and no, they weren't.

"Just about. What time is it?"Grant asked, rubbing his eyes and looking over at Jamie who'd just rolled over and opened his pretty blue eyes. For a second, Grant got lost in them. Lord, they'd torn it up last night. He figured he might be sore as soon as he started moving around this morning. Figured Jamie might be, too. But it was a good sore and well worth it. Jamie smiled at him.

"Good night, I take it. Well, Mark and I are on our way over. We'll do the payback thing. You all want doughnuts or breakfast biscuits?" Wade said.

"You don't have to do that—"

"Just pick."

"Biscuits." Grant said. He grinned as Wade hung up.

"Biscuits?" Jamie asked, yawning and stretching. Grant could tell when Jamie realised that he might be a little bit achy in some places.

"You a little tender there, too?" Jamie teased. "That was Officer Wade. They're on their way over here to check out the fence, I guess. He's bringing breakfast to pay us back for last night. Guess I'll make some coffee. We need to get the ladder out of the utility room. I bet they'll need it."

"Okay, but first, bathroom and a good morning kiss, hug, something. I mean, it's Sunday. If I have to be up and about, at least I should be happy about it." Jamie acted as if he were complaining, but Grant could tell he was teasing. Jamie wasn't lazy and didn't sleep in very often.

Grant rolled to pull Jamie into a good hard hug then turned to get up.

"Come on, bathroom, brush teeth then super kiss. We need one that will last a while since we won't get to indulge in our usual Sunday routine." Grant reached to pull Jamie up with him. Jamie had already scooted over to Grant's side of the bed and was ready to be tugged up beside Grant.

They stumbled into the bathroom together, taking care of business, and before long leaned on the counter, thoroughly involved in the aforementioned super kiss. Grant made sure it was long, wet and passionate. Jamie's stomach rumbled, breaking them into laughter or the kiss would probably have still been going on when the policemen got there.

They were dressed and ready when the doorbell rang. Grant opened it to Wade with a bag and a container with four big orange juices. Oh, yum. With that and the coffee, they'd all be floating, but it looked great.

"I bet it's not everybody that gets this kind of service from the force," he teased Wade.

"You got that right. Uh, you all have more trouble last night? You've got a nasty looking bruise on your neck there," Wade teased him. Grant's hand went to the spot under his ear that Jamie had licked and sucked and nibbled on last night. Grant blushed and Wade laughed out loud. Grant reached out like he was going to punch his shoulder, but since it had an official looking patch on it, he drew back.

"Oh, go ahead. I'm here as much as a friend as I am an officer this morning. You know you want to take a whack at me," Wade teased.

Jamie came in just then and said, "What's this? Grant, you're attacking a police officer in our living room? I can see the eleven o'clock news now." Officer Thomas, who'd been quiet until now, laughed at that.

"Come on back to the kitchen, and we'll enjoy this breakfast you brought. There's even some brownies left. Biscuits and orange juice followed by coffee and brownies. Breakfast of champions, for sure. Works for me." Jamie led the way, and they all followed, each nodding in agreement.

Grant set out dishes and they all sat around the table, eating quickly and talking about what they were going to do.

"This feels like a drama on TV instead of my life," Grant said. "It feels weird to be having breakfast and talking with the officers on our case. There's not any reason this shouldn't be happening, is there?"

"Not really. You're right. It's not normal procedure, but it's not illegal. If you were the bad guys and we were sharing information, it might be looked at as a problem, but I think we're good. Unless it really bothers you. Does it?" Wade asked, looking at Grant.

"No, not at all. Seriously, I think it's great. I'd say it could only help our case that you have a vested interest in keeping your friends safe," Grant teased. He knew Wade Johnson by now. He knew every case would get the attention they were getting, just not the personal aspect of it.

"Yeah, that's it. How about you, Mark? You in this for the brownies and the buddy system?" Wade asked his partner.

"It's a new take on the job, but I could get used to it." Mark Thomas smiled back at Wade, and Grant suddenly had a revelation, a feeling. Mark Thomas was in love with Wade Johnson. Then it hit him. Oh, man, that sucks. Wade was straight. Grant had never even thought about Thomas, one way or the other, but once the idea occurred to him, it wouldn't go away. He was going to talk to Jamie about this.

"Jamie's going to get the ladder for you all. How do you want to do this? How can we help?" Grant asked.

"You all said your neighbours back there were gone for a while? That could explain why no one has seen him. Some of this has been done in the light of day, so he got lucky in that they have a fence around their property, too, and the tree is a big spreading one. Grant, why don't you come with us over to that side, and Jamie, you stay over here on this side of the fence. You can slide the ladder up over the top to us on that side, but first I want to see if there's any evidence over there." Wade was back in Officer Johnson mode, and they all set to following his instructions.

Soon, Grant stood with the two officers looking at the fence from the other side. Grant knew that Jamie and Brit were opposite them. The three of them looked closely at this side of the fence, but there didn't seem to be any markings, especially ones that said in any way, *"I used this spot to go over."*

Jamie's voice came over, "You all see anything?" Brit's voice was heard next with a single bark. That got a laugh from all of them.

"No, nothing, Jamie," Grant said. "Wade, you want the ladder now? I think if we put it on the fence, up close, and you all hold it, with my height I could see the limb closer. It won't matter if I touch it or hang onto it, will it? I mean you're not going to find prints up there, are you?"

"Yeah, no problem. Jamie! Can you start the ladder over the fence? We'll get it as it comes over here."

Grant watched as the ladder cleared the top of the fence and the two officers grabbed it on its way down. They put it against the fence and made sure it was set firmly. Grant started up and soon was looking down at Jamie on the other side.

"Hello there, Handsome."

"Hey, that's Willie's name for me. You have to come up with your own," Grant teased him.

"You don't really want me to go through the list now, do you?" Jamie shot back.

Grant knew he was blushing as he replied, "No, not now. Hold on, guys, I'm going to stand up on the top of it. Damn, I don't see how anybody could get on that limb to…whoa, back up. I take it back." Grant steadied himself by putting his palms against the side of the limb for balance.

"The top of the limb is really messed up. I mean the bark is all scraped off of it. I can see it clearly. I bet you could see it, Mark, if you came up here. Hold it, I'm coming back down. You all know more about this kind of thing, but it looks like something's been on that limb." Grant started backing down the ladder and felt better when he could grasp the sides and hurried to the bottom.

Mark took his place and scuttled up the ladder. Grant turned to watch Wade as he eyed Mark's progress. Wade's eyes were square on Mark's behind, and Grant had that feeling again, but his time, it was about Wade. No way. Wasn't Wade straight? Why would he be checking out Mark's admittedly nice ass? He was really going to have to talk to Jamie about this.

"Be careful," Grant said, knowing that when Mark got to the top of the ladder, he'd have to grab for the limb, not being as tall as Grant was. Mark reached for the limb with one hand and with the other he pulled a camera out of his shirt pocket. He whistled as he took shot after shot of the top side of the limb.

"Grant's right. Something has torn the bark off the top of this limb. My guess is repeated used of a rope. If I could just reach a little further, I could see if there are any fibres left up here. There have to be. Jamie," Mark said, looking down into their yard, "can you get me a wet towel from the kitchen, preferably a light coloured one?"

"Sure. Be right back," Grant heard Jamie say. And he was.

Jamie put the towel on top of the fence and Grant took it down. Grant very carefully started up the ladder to pass it up to Mark. Mark flipped it over the limb and pulled, dragging it across. As it came down he passed it down to Grant, who passed it to Wade. Wade folded it with the debris on the inside.

"Good enough, Mark. Come on down. Be careful." Grant had backed off the ladder carefully so as not to jar it. He held the sides as Mark started down. Mark was on the third rung when his heel slipped and he started to fall backwards.

"Whoa! Wade!" Mark yelled for help as he lost his balance. Grant stepped over quickly, but Wade was faster. He caught Mark as he was just about horizontal. If he'd gone down further, he'd have caught his foot between the rungs and probably broken something. Grant grabbed hold of Mark's arm, helping Wade hold him as he tried to get his foot free. It happened in seconds. Soon, Mark stood beside them, breathing hard.

From the other side of the fence, Jamie yelled, "What happened? Is everybody okay? Hello?"

Grant answered him with, "It's all good. Mark almost fell, but we caught him."

Grant turned back around to see Wade looking at Mark...and Mark looking at Wade. There was that feeling again.

"You're okay, right, Mark?" he asked, breaking the moment.

"Yeah, fine. Thanks, both of you. I'm just clumsy, I guess," Mark said.

Wade looked down at the towel he still had in his hand. Grant saw him take a deep breath and seemed to shake off the moment.

"So tell me about these neighbours, Grant. They're in Europe, right? When are they due back?"

"Uh, in about five weeks I think. They're nice people. Why?"

"Just a thought. I'll have to think about it some more. We've got what we need for this morning. Let's go back over and talk to Jamie. Mark and I are going to see what we can find out about the coach's movements." They passed the ladder back to Jamie and headed back.

They met back at Grant and Jamie's house and soon the officers had gone on with their investigation and Jamie and Grant had the rest of the day ahead of them. The first thing Grant wanted to do was talk to Jamie.

As they shared kitchen duty, Grant asked, "Hey, did you notice anything different about Wade and Mark?"

"You mean other than the fact that we're calling them by their first names all of a sudden? That feels weird, but I really like them. What do you mean?" Jamie stopped drying the cups and turned to Grant.

Grant finished rinsing the sink and turned off the water. Facing Jamie, he leant back on the counter and crossed his arms over his chest.

"I think that Mark's in love with Wade."

"Hmm? You think...wait, but Wade's straight. He was married. That would make it really suck for Mark. What makes you think so?" Jamie looked contemplative.

"I saw Mark looking at Wade in here this morning, and I just had a feeling, a fleeting thought. Then later, I caught a look on Wade's face and had the same feeling."

"What? You think Wade might have feelings for Mark, too?" Jamie looked sceptical.

Grant nodded and clarified with, "Then after Mark fell, and we caught him there was a moment when they were looking at each other. I tell you I could feel the vibes. It was just for a second, but I could swear to it."

"I don't know what to think. If they do have feelings for each other, I hope they can work them out, one way or the other. If Wade is straight, Mark's in for a world of hurt. And if he's gay, or at least bi, I hope they can get it together. We'll just be friends and be here for them either way. They're working hard for us, helping us, and going the extra bit to do it. We'll see." Jamie spread his arms and motioned for Grant to come into them.

Grant settled against him and said, "I just hate for one or both of them to be hurt."

"I know, baby. Maybe it'll turn out okay. We can't do anything about it except be their friends. Come on, what do you want to do the rest of the day?"

"I want to go somewhere with you and Brit. Let's get in the truck and go to the lake. It's not that far. We'll take some stuff for a picnic supper and just play all day. We can swim, play on the beach, take a Frisbee, couple of lawn chairs. I just want to get out of here. What do you think?" Grant leant back in Jamie's arms and looked at him.

"I think that's a great idea. Brit would love it and so would I. Let's go play. Well, first, another super kiss. I liked that one this morning, but it's worn off."

Grant went right for Jamie's mouth, no hesitation. Jamie opened to him, and Grant thrust his tongue inside, meeting and mating with Jamie's. Putting his arms around Jamie's neck, he held on and sunk into the kiss. Resting his stomach against Jamie's, he luxuriated in the feel of their bodies meeting. Jamie's body was home to him. The way they fit together and melded into one being with torsos plastered together, arms and legs entwined, made him feel like he was where he was meant to be.

"Grant, I love the way you feel in my arms," Jamie murmured against his neck when they finally pulled their lips apart. Grant wasn't surprised that Jamie had said what he'd been thinking. It made sense to him.

"I know, love, me, too." Grant held onto Jamie for a few more seconds before pulling away.

"Okay, you want to cook out at one of the grills they have there or just take sandwiches and chips, drinks and brownies?" Grant asked, going to the refrigerator.

"Sandwiches and chips sounds good. I'll get the stuff we'll need for Brit. This is a good idea. We need to get away from all this."

* * * *

It was a tired group that headed for the back door later that night. They had played and romped on the beach. They'd swum in the lake, eaten their sandwiches and polished off the rest of the brownies. Brit had pretty much won the Frisbee game and made friends with every person he saw on the beach. It had, in Grant's mind, been a perfect day.

Brit started barking and there went the calm peaceful feeling their day out together had generated. Pawing at the door and growling, Brit seemed to be pushing for them to hurry.

"Uh, Grant, I don't *think* we left the kitchen light on. Hell, it looks like every light in the house is on. How'd we miss that when we drove up?" Jamie asked, trying the door without the key first, and turning to look at Grant when it opened.

Grant knew what that look was. He knew they had locked the door and could kick himself because they hadn't gone and gotten the deadbolts like they should have. Maybe they needed an alarm system, too.

"We were talking and tired and not paying attention. Should we go in, or call the police first?" Grant was wondering aloud.

"Might as well go in. Brit's already doing his furious scan of the house. I doubt if there's anyone in here now. Come on," Jamie motioned. They carried in their supplies and set them on the table.

"Something's bothering me," Jamie said, walking through the house with Grant right beside him.

"What's that? Besides the obvious, I mean," Grant asked.

"I saw this coach, Gilbert, right? He doesn't look like the kind of man who can throw a rope over a tree limb, climb up, and swing over into our yard and then back. Does he to you?"

"Now that you mention it, no. I mean, he's not fat and lazy, but he's not in prime condition either. That's a good thought. Of course, it just muddies the water more. If it's not him, then who?" Grant threw that lovely thought out there.

"Damn, you're right. This just gets weirder all the time." Jamie said, as they came back to the kitchen.

They worked in tandem to clean up and put away the things from their trip. Silence reigned for a few minutes as they were both thinking about the things they'd talked about. Grant had just decided that they ought to call Wade and get his input on the latest and the thoughts Jamie had brought up.

"Maybe it's time to call Wade again, even if it's just to tell him what we think. I don't think there's anything to find this time, but if he finds that coach, he might be able to think about whether he thinks the coach could do the Tarzan thing with the rope." Jamie looked at Grant with a question in his eyes when he saw Grant shaking his head. "What?"

"I was just thinking the same thing. Another example of our thinking alike, that's all." Grant handed the phone to Jamie and pulled out a chair at the table. Jamie took another one and they waited for the call to go through at the police station.

Jamie requested to speak to Officer Johnson and was told that he was out on a case. Jamie asked if he could leave a message for the officer to call him when he returned as what he was calling about was not an emergency. Given the go-ahead, he asked for the officer to call them before he went home that night.

"I guess we wait to hear from him. Let's try to think of anyone else who might be doing this stuff to us. If they find the coach, and he's not our guy, then who would do this? It's personal, Grant. The writing of the note, that's personal. I mean, sure, whoever broke in and went through our stuff could find the notes and make one up, but it's an in-your-face kind of gesture. The others are just hassling, terrorising type things, but that one...weird. With that, he got into our personal life." Jamie reached for Grant's hand and linked their fingers.

Grant agreed with Jamie, and it made him shiver. It made sense, and Grant had to admit to himself that he hadn't gone there with his thoughts. Maybe because it was just too scary.

"Jamie, the only time I've ever been this scared and this freaked out was last year when Donnie was doing his evil thing. I don't like feeling fear. I mean, I really don't like being afraid all the time that something worse is going to happen. I'm going to go to work tomorrow and worry about what is happening here or with you or Brit. This sucks."

"I know, baby. I feel the same way. At least, I'm on vacation as of Wednesday for a full eleven days. I'm going to start on the deck. They're bringing the supplies over Tuesday afternoon." Jamie played with Grant's fingers as he talked. "I've got a couple of the guys helping me get started with the framing. Jim's coming and bringing a few of his crew to get us started. I met Jim through Tony, and he's a nice guy. He's head of a construction crew. After the frame is up, I can work on it for a while. Jim said he'd check in each night and give advice or help until we get to the part where we need more skilled workers in." Jamie said, sounding excited about the upcoming project.

"I wish I could get off to help you, but this is not a good time for vacations in the parks department." Grant pulled Jamie's hand up to his mouth, just pressing it to his lips.

"I know, but it's the only time I could get off, and we want to get it done. Another plus is the weather is supposed to be good all week. We'll plan a deck-raisin' like they did for barns in the old days. We'll invite all our friends and have a big push to get it done while I'm off. Maybe you can help me a little at night when you get in. I know you'll be tired, but I want you to feel part of it all." Jamie squeezed Grant's hand, smiling when Grant pressed right back. Their hands were making subtle love, their fingers moving in and out and around each others. Their palms would meet and mash together then go back to sliding into the finger clutch again.

"I want to. It'll be fine. We'll get some time together to work on it. I'm looking forward to using the things we've planned for out there. Besides that, I'm looking forward to inviting Wade to join us. What about Mark? He's been a part of all this. I don't want to seem like I'm trying to meddle and provide them with opportunities to be together, you know?" Grant said.

Grant raised his eyebrows when he felt Jamie pulling him forward. He got up and went with the tugs and ended up in Jamie's lap again. He knew it had to look goofy with his long legs and arms, sitting with his head high above Jamie's. But with Jamie's arms around him, he didn't care what it looked like. He bent to take Jamie's lips in a soft kiss.

"Hello there," Jamie said, "I like you on my lap. You are my big guy, aren't you? As soon as we hear back from our officer friend, I want to shower with you. We'll get the lake water and sand off, and I'll make your skin shine and your eyes glow. As for our friends, they can find opportunities to be together away from work without counting on us, so we can invite them without worrying about it being considered meddling."

"You're right. I may even be reading things into a couple of looks that just aren't really there. I like the sound of your plan, though. Wonder when they'll call?" Grant said, leaning down and putting his forehead to Jamie's.

Jamie tilted his head so they could press more than their heads together. The kiss started out slowly, with Grant's tongue tracing Jamie's lips before pushing inside. Jamie opened his mouth and invited Grant right in. Grant slid his tongue over Jamie's teeth, engaged his tongue in a duel then flicked it against the roof of Jamie's mouth. As expected, Jamie pulled back, laughing. For some reason, that spot was ticklish for Jamie, and Grant went for it every once in a while.

"Stop that. Come back here," Jamie said, reaching up and cupping the side of Grant's head, pulling it back down to his. "I don't care when they call. I'm a little preoccupied. Kiss now," he ordered, and Grant was happy to comply, bending again and not teasing this time.

This kiss went straight to passion, bypassing any teasing or foreplay. Jamie opened wide and Grant took advantage of his position to tilt Jamie's head back, taking his mouth with hunger. Jamie's fingers were now moving on Grant's head, taking the band out of his hair and calling up goose bumps as his fingers moved over Grant's scalp.

"Mmm, getting hard for you, Jamie. We're starting something we might have to stop when the phone rings. God, I love you. Wait, here..." Grant stood up, and turned to straddle Jamie in his chair. Their groins were pressed together, both hard and now grinding together. Grant went right back to Jamie's mouth, despite his worry that they would be interrupted.

Grant had enjoyed their day off together so much. It had been a rude awakening to come home and find they'd been broken into again. He wanted to just forget it all and spend some quality time with his love, his Jamie. This embrace was his need for Jamie and his small act of rebellion against what was happening. He wrapped his arms around Jamie's neck and held on, kissing Jamie with passion and hunger, sweeping through Jamie's mouth.

Jamie wasn't quiescent during the clinch. His hands were moving over Grant's head and his back. Grant couldn't help the shiver that swept over his body as Jamie's hands moved over him. He loved doing everything with Jamie, but he absolutely adored being intimate with him. The softness, tenderness and gentleness they often shared meant the world to him. The fire, passion and hunger they indulged in took his breath away. Grant blessed the day that Jamie walked into his room at the rehab centre last year.

"I'm so in love with you, Jamie Taylor," Grant managed to say when Jamie finally pulled his mouth away and put it in Grant's neck.

"God, Grant, I know you are. That means everything to me. I love you so much, and it just grows more every day. I just want us to be able to live and love and be happy together without all this drama. Case in point, I want to be able to take you to bed right now without having to wait to report the latest situation. We're waiting to talk to the police instead of sharing our time making love before we have to go back to work tomorrow. I sound whiny, don't I?" Jamie looked rueful, as he put his head to Grant's chest.

"You're just saying what I'm thinking, so don't worry about it." Grant bent to take Jamie's lips again when Brit went flying by them headed for the back door, barking ferociously, scaring the crap out of Grant.

Chapter Eight

"What? Brit! What is it?" Grant moved off Jamie, standing and moving with him to the door to see what had Brit so upset. Brit barked and pawed and acted, well, just like he had been recently. Jamie opened the door and started out but stopped dead in his tracks.

"Shit! Brit! Stop, come back here. Right now, Brit. Here, now!"

Grant was freaking out because he couldn't see what had Jamie so disturbed. Brit was growling and snarling and wasn't obeying Jamie, and Grant had never known that to happen.

"Jamie, what the hell?" Grant finally demanded since Jamie was blocking the door, trying to get Brit back in and keep Grant from going out.

"Call the cops, Grant, hurry. Tell them to bring animal control. There's a rattlesnake on the patio, and he's not happy."

"A rattler? Damn! I'm calling. You stay away from him, Jamie. Get Brit and get back in here. Please, baby, please." In between Brit's barks, Grant could now hear the rattling sound that warned of imminent danger with this particular threat.

"Hello. This is an emergency. This is Grant Stevens calling. I need to know how to get animal control to come to my house. Yes, that's the address. Someone has put a rattlesnake on our patio. No sir, we're not outside with it. We're trying to get the dog inside, but he wants out there. Also, we need to see if Officer Johnson is there yet. He is? Please, put him on. He's working on our case." Before he could give him the address, Wade was on the line.

"Oh God, Wade, please get animal control here. There's a rattlesnake on the patio right by the back door. Brit's going crazy, and Jamie's trying to get him back in here before he gets bitten. Okay. Yes, sir. Okay, I will. Please hurry." Grant dropped the phone onto the table and hurried to the utility room, grabbing a broom and a rake that was hanging there.

"Jamie here, Wade said to use this to keep him back from us. Can't you get Brit to come in?" Grant was trying to get Jamie out of the way, give him the rake and see Brit at the same time.

"No, he thinks he's protecting us and he won't come. Brit, come on, boy. Come here, now! Shit, Grant if he gets bitten I'm gonna kill somebody. Stay back, Brit. Leave it alone." Jamie sounded so agitated and worried. Grant tried to pull him out of the doorway.

"Jamie, I want to see. I want to help. Between us, we can make sure it doesn't get to Brit. Wade said to use these to keep it back from us." Grant understood Jamie wanting to protect him but he felt the same way about Jamie. He wanted him away from danger and safe inside.

"I'm sorry, Grant. God, baby, be careful." Instead of coming back inside, Jamie edged out to the right of the door, letting Grant see clearly for the first time.

Brit was standing in front of a huge rattlesnake that was coiled up, head rocking, and tail shaking and making that eerie noise. Grant took his courage in hand and edged out to the left of the door, somehow having the presence of mind to flip on the outside light and close the door as he did. They certainly didn't want that thing inside the house. Grant knew if Brit wasn't coming in, then Jamie wasn't and by the same token, neither was he.

"Wonder how long it will take them to get here? Wade had just gotten there and was going to call us. He's getting animal control over here, and he said he and Mark would be here as fast as they could. Not fast enough, man. This seriously freaks me out. I ever tell you I'm scared shitless of snakes?" Grant admitted, the broom held out in front of him.

"No, and now isn't a good time, either. You could have stayed in there," Jamie said, all the while moving slowly, keeping his eyes on the snake that was still rattling and sticking that tongue out.

"Why are you moving?" Grant whispered.

"Why are you whispering? He can't hear you. I don't want it to get away. If it feels vibrations from different areas, it won't leave. I just don't want Brit too close. He's minding by staying back from it, but I'll feel better when the guys with the know-how get here," Jamie said, stopping for a moment.

"You're not that scared, are you? My brave guy," Grant said, standing still, back against the wall, broom out in front of him.

"No, I'm not really. I just don't want anyone hurt. You're brave, too, you know?"

"Uh-huh. I'm not sure I didn't just pee in my pants," Grant said, trying to make light and not show how scared he really was.

"You're out here, despite your fear, because all that you love is out here. That's bravery, Grant. I love you so much."

Jamie was actually declaring his love with a rattlesnake clattering in the background. How bizarre was this night? Brit had stopped his frantic barking and had settled for a near constant low growl that was nearly as eerie as the rattle from the reptile.

Finally, they heard tires squealing and doors slamming. He glanced over to the left, waiting for them to show up through the gate. There were two men obviously from animal control in the front with long sticks with hooks on the end, a burlap sack and a box. Behind them came Officers Johnson and Thomas. Grant finally breathed again.

"Hi, guys." Grant hoped his total fear and sissyness didn't show in his voice.

"Hey. Jamie, Grant, you all just stand still now. Let these two take care of things. Jamie, can you get Brit to back off now?" Wade asked as the four men eased up to the patio.

"Brit, here boy. It's okay now. Come here, *now*." Jamie had put the end of his rake down and slapped his thigh and Brit looked over at the men approaching then looked at Jamie. Brit stopped growling and came right over to Jamie. Grant breathed another sigh of relief.

Grant started edging towards the back door but stopped when the snake turned its head towards him and leant forward. His ability to breathe left him right then.

"Still, Grant. Very still," Wade said. Grant knew his eyes were huge as he watched the two men step confidently towards the snake. One hooked the middle of the snake, while the other aimed for the head, trapping it in the crook and taking it to the ground. Somehow they manoeuvred around to where the snake was stretched out. The first guy opened the bag he still held. He bent and slid it under the still rapidly rattling tail and slid it up, while the other man held the head down on the ground.

The whole time the snake was wiggling and trying to get loose, but couldn't get away. The guy holding the head down moved around to where he stood in front of the head and the other man just pulled the bag up past the head and closed the sack and lifted it. They could all see the angry snake striking out at the sides of the bag over and over. The other man slowly and carefully drew the hooked stick out of the bag without causing the top to open. A collective sigh was heard and awkward laughter followed.

"Thanks, guys. Feel free to go ahead and box that thing up and lock it, if you don't mind. We'll take it from here," Wade said. The two men put the still-moving bag into the box, closed the lid and locked it down. As they stood to leave with it, Grant stepped forward on shaky legs and shook both their hands.

"Thank you so much. I will freely admit I could not have done that. Sorry to have bothered you tonight."

Jamie came over and added his thanks and even Brit barked and nudged each man's free hand for a welcome pat from them. This got a more relieved laugh and the AC guys left the way they'd come. The four remaining men looked at each other for a moment, each probably thinking the same thing. This was getting dangerous. No one believed that snake had just shown up on their property. Who knew how long it had been in the yard? It certainly wasn't on the patio when they'd come in. Grant really needed Jamie's arms around him right now. But he was a man, so he tried to act like one.

"Come on in, guys. I don't know if there's any way you can look for any kind of evidence tonight. I'll make coffee. Sorry, we finished off the brownies at the lake today."

"You two go on in and take Brit. I don't think there's anything else out here or he wouldn't be calm now. We're going to check it out, though. Jamie, you might need to calm this one down." Wade pointed at Grant.

"What gave me away?" Grant asked, ruefully.

"You haven't stopped shaking yet, and I'm not sure he's going to be able to get that broom away from you," Wade teased, gently. "Go on. We'll be right in."

Grant headed for the back door, glad to get the chance. He hoped Jamie and Brit were following. He could hear Jamie praising Brit as they all poured into the kitchen. Jamie took the broom from Grant and put both weapons up. He got down a treat for Brit then tugged Grant over past the refrigerator and up against the counter. Grant finally got his wish.

Jamie grabbed the front of Grant's shirt and pulled him up tight against him. He plundered his mouth with a deeply penetrating tongue. Grant whimpered into his mouth, needing more, needing Jamie. He wrapped his arms around Jamie and held on tight, meeting Jamie's tongue with his and breathing deep. He wanted to inhale Jamie and eat him up all at once. Grant knew they didn't have but a few minutes, but he couldn't let Jamie go. Wade was right. Grant couldn't stop shaking. He realised that his hair was still down from where Jamie had been playing in it before. There were more bands in the bathroom. But that would require that he move away from Jamie.

Jamie finally pulled back and looked at him, blue eyes on blue. Jamie's heart was in his eyes, and Grant couldn't look away.

"I love you. We'll continue this later. Why don't you go and clean up? I'll make the coffee, maybe pull down some Pop-Tarts, huh? You did great, baby. Really."

Grant had to take another kiss, but he finally pulled back and turned to do as Jamie suggested. He wished he had time for that shower now. But he went in, combed and tied back his hair, and quickly washed his face. Rejoining Jamie in the kitchen, he was just in time to help put out creamer, sugar, and the coffee mugs. Jamie had gotten down the Frosted Cherry Pop Tarts as he'd mentioned and was heating them in the toaster oven. They agreed that the treats were much better warm. Jamie put four out on a dessert plate just as Wade and Mark came in.

"You all are spoiling us. We don't get this treatment anywhere else," Wade said, pulling out a chair and putting his ever-present tablet on the table. Mark Thomas took the chair next to him and Jamie filled all their mugs. Grant sat in one of the other chairs, and Jamie surprised him by pulling the last one over to put it right beside him. Under the table, Jamie took his hand and linked their fingers. Grant's heart turned over at the gesture.

Jamie knew that Grant was still rattled. *No pun intended*, he thought, smiling just a little. Jamie didn't care how it looked in front of their friends, he was going to supply the support and comfort that Grant needed right now. Grant had never loved him so much as right now. Their friends knew they were lovers, but Jamie and Grant never threw it in their faces. Jamie was thinking only of Grant and his need for a bit of normalcy. Grant had an almost uncontrollable urge to kiss the man right in front of the two officers.

Wade smiled at them but said nothing. He glanced over at Mark, though, setting off Grant's gaydar again. Grant schooled his face so as not to show his thoughts. Jamie squeezed his hand, and Grant took that to mean he'd noticed the same glance.

"As expected, we didn't find anything else back there, but we did look carefully. I don't think any of us believe that rattlesnake just showed up here in your backyard. They're not that uncommon in this area, but to find one in town, on your patio, not normal at all. This is getting dangerous, boys. And by the way, what was your call about earlier?" Wade asked, breaking off a corner of his pastry and nibbling.

"We went to the lake and spent the whole day after you all left here. When we returned home, Brit went wild again, wanting in. We noticed that all lights were on though we hadn't left any on, and the door was unlocked again," Jamie said.

"You should—"

"Have gotten the deadbolts you told us to get. Yes sir, I know. I thought of that just as we realised that the door was unlocked tonight. We just tore out of here this morning, wanting to get away from everything. We completely forgot about the new locks. Think we ought to go to one of the all-night stores and get some tonight?" Just the thought had Grant cringeing. That would mean hours before they could sleep.

"I doubt if he'll do anything else tonight. Just lock up and leave the outside lights on. Was that all you wanted earlier, to tell us about the door and the lights?" Wade asked.

"That, and to ask if you'd gotten anywhere on the Coach Gilbert front." Grant went on to tell them what he and Jamie had discussed about the coach's probable inability to do the stunts necessary.

"Well, I haven't seen the man yet, but if you say so, I'll take your word for it. That leaves us with a big question. I'll still try to find this coach, but if you don't like him for the rope trick, we're looking at someone else. Any idea who else has a hard-on for you all? Uh, I didn't mean it like that."

Jamie and Grant both laughed at Wade's embarrassment.

"We've already talked about that. About who else would want to hurt us and the only other person we know of is Donnie, and he's in prison for another four years. Right? He couldn't be out, could he?" That's the first time that Grant had actually said it out loud and just saying the words had his heart accelerating.

"I doubt that. With him getting five years, one year would be way too early for getting out on good behaviour. I can't see how he'd manage it. I'll make a few calls and see what I can find out tomorrow. No other ideas?" Wade asked, making notes in his pad.

"We're not really the type to make a lot of enemies at the rehab centre or the parks department. The coach thing was a first for me," Grant said.

"So now we have to wonder if any of it was done by Gilbert, the scratches on the truck and all the other stuff. I don't really see him doing the note, do you, Grant? That sounds more like something Donnie would do." Grant jerked his head around to Jamie at the ease with which Jamie made that statement.

"You think it's him, maybe? God, I'm just not ready to think that," Grant said, sitting back in his chair.

"Would you rather think there's someone else who hates us this much?" Jamie asked.

"No, but Donnie tried to *kill* people." Grant was afraid his whine was showing now.

"And that snake could have done the job tonight. So, we're back to square one." Jamie pulled on Grant's hand and their shoulders bumped. Grant leaned in, needing the contact.

"Okay, I've got this report done on the break-in tonight. Nothing taken, just lights left on and door open. Then the snake's appearance and retrieval. I'd suggest you all shop early in the morning, get the locks, and put them on before you go in to work. Both of you, together, so you have keys. Get extra made while you're there. If you don't mind, I'd like to have one. We'll make some drive-bys when we can until we get this figured out. If I see something suspicious, do I have your permission to come in?"

"Hell, yes. Just be careful. You're considered a friend now, so I'll give you a key based on that. The fact that you're on our case makes it doubly smart. How will we get it to you?"

"I'll come by the centre tomorrow after I do some more checking on the coach. You can give it to me then. Give me your cell numbers, so I can get to you in a hurry if I need to. Be sure they are always charged so we can stay in contact. In the meantime, I'll also see what I can find out about Donnie Wilkins."

"God, just the fact that you are saying that sends chills down my spine," Grant said.

"What do you say we have a meeting here tomorrow night when we get off work? We'll go over what we've found out and see about making some plans for safety."

Jamie and Grant agreed to that and told them that Jamie was going on vacation Wednesday. Now that Grant thought about that, he wasn't sure he wanted Jamie here by himself all day working outside with someone out to do them harm.

"Do you think it's safe for Jamie to be working here alone out back all day with this person free to do who knows what to him? It worries me." Grant didn't want to imply that Jamie couldn't take care of himself, but this whole thing had him shaken.

"Maybe I'll see if Jim knows of anybody in his crew who's looking for some extra work. It'll make the work get done faster, and it will relieve your mind, huh?" Jamie said, turning to look in Grant's eyes.

Grant just nodded, knowing his heart was in his eyes.

"That's it then. I'm not crazy about being up on a ladder with no one around and somebody showing up to cause trouble. I'll have someone with me, and we'll be aware at all times."

"I had a thought," Mark Thomas said, finally joining the conversation.

"What's that?" Wade asked.

"The tree limb is clearly sticking way out over your property. I think it would be within your rights to cut the limb down. I don't know how you feel about doing it while your neighbours are out of town, but I think you'd have legality on your side if they fought it."

"I don't think they'd fight it. We've talked about it and decided it wasn't bothering anything back there, and we'd even thought about putting some chairs back there in the shade. We could do without it. It would cut off an avenue he's using to get in here. Make it a little harder for him. What do you think, Grant?" Jamie asked his opinion, still holding his hand.

"It's a shame to cut that big, old limb. I doubt if they would care, especially when they find out why. What if we put something back there that would make him think twice about jumping down into our yard?"

"Like what?" Jamie asked, head tilted.

"My first thought was green paint. Just paint the grass with oil base paint with maybe some extra oil in it so it wouldn't dry and when he hops down he'd be covered in it, maybe even slide around a little. If he gets it on his hands he'd have a hard time going back up the rope. Kind of like they put the ink dyes in the money when they do a sting on TV. Or, hey, what about we pepper the area with nails and tacks and spikes and just wait for him to impale himself?"

"Now you're thinking like one of the bad guys. That's pretty smart. We may resort to something like that. Let's see if he tries anything with someone here all day. That might slow him down. So far, it's been little things, but I do see a definite escalation," Wade said, sitting back.

"I think we need to have a cookout here on Tuesday night and invite Tony, Jim and his crew that will be helping. Wade, you and Mark are invited to come by, too. Are you on or off then?"

"We're both on, but we could come by for supper and a strategy session. We have to eat, and we can do both that way. We're both off on Friday. I'd be glad to come by and help on the deck. How about you, Mark, you doing anything Friday?"

Mark shook his head and just like that it was decided. They were having a cookout Tuesday night, and they had more help on Friday. Grant would see if he could get the day off. Maybe he could trade off with someone else. He'd keep it a surprise until he found out.

* * * *

Finally, Grant was headed to the bedroom, his arm around Jamie, determined that nothing was going to get between them now. Grant was nearly dropping with exhaustion, but he intended to have that shower with Jamie and couldn't wait to get to the bed and hold him tight. If they both had the energy for more, so be it, but he needed to be with Jamie now, and to feel safe.

"Been a hell of a day, huh, baby?" Jamie said, walking with Grant right into the bathroom. It looked like Jamie was ready for that shared shower, too.

"I thought I was through living in fear of what was going to happen next. I hate this, Jamie. I want to just be happy with you. No! That's enough!"

Jamie looked shocked at Grant's about face from quietly upset to aggressive and firm.

"Grant?"

"I'm sorry, but I'm done for the night. No more talking about it. I want the rest of the night to be just for us, you and me. It seems like forever since we were free to just be together. Today at the lake was fun, and I enjoyed it, but the situation was never far from my mind. Now I want to do something to take our minds off everything but how much we're in love and how we can make each other feel."

Grant started removing Jamie's clothes with a no-nonsense fervour. Jamie caught on and did the same for Grant. In seconds, they were naked and embracing. Grant took the band out of his hair and shook his head. Instead of taking things further, he pulled Jamie to the shower and turned it on. He was flat-out taking over, a man with a mission.

"I think I like you like this," Jamie said, closing them in and reaching for Grant.

Grant put his arms around Jamie and moved so that they each were in and out of the stream of water. He grabbed the shampoo and handed it to Jamie. In seconds, there were goose bumps all over his body as Jamie worked the thick gel all through his hair, scratching his scalp and massaging the nape of his neck. Grant grabbed some and reached up to reciprocate. They rinsed under the spray then began the enjoyable task of bathing each other.

Grant began by sudsing the loofah and caressing Jamie from head to toe, leaving not an inch untouched. Certain areas he reserved for his fingers, being gentle and teasing. When Jamie took over and more or less mirrored Grant's actions, Grant stood as still as he could through each caress, though Jamie cheated and interspersed his strokes with kisses.

Grant let it all go. He did. Feelings of intimacy and being away from everything evil and safe in their own world made it all go away for him. As soon as they stood, both completely clean, Grant turned Jamie to put his back to the wall. His mind went back to the time when they first started out together, and he'd had Jamie up against the wall in the bedroom and blew his mind. Knowing he wouldn't have as much time to play as he had then before the water got cold, he still went for it.

Thrusting his hands through his hair and pushing the wet strands out of his face, he looked at Jamie, slowly up and down, head to toe. Jamie wasn't the least bit slow, and it was clear that he remembered and was happy to re-enact the scene. Grant moved right into Jamie, plastering himself to Jamie's body, his head bent to Jamie's neck. Very gently, he traced across the top of Jamie's shoulder and down to his right nipple. He licked and sucked until Jamie gasped, but he didn't move, knowing from before that Grant didn't want him to.

Grant was not as thorough as he'd been last year, but he certainly made his point. He worshipped Jamie's body with a single-minded drive that had Jamie shaking and begging Grant to end his agony. His cock was hard against Grant's stomach when Grant stood back up. Grant took pity on him and ground against him, his cock rubbing on Jamie's and they both groaned.

"Ah, Grant, please, baby. I'm not going to be able to stand up here much longer. You are so good at this, this build up, but please do something." Jamie's hands were flat against the wall by his hips but the muscles in his arms stood out.

Grant leant in to kiss him quickly not wanting to get into more here. He turned and shut off the water, opening the door and pulling Jamie out with him. Jamie must have decided the scene was over because he took over now. Grabbing a towel, he proceeded to dry Grant's body in such a way as to insure that he stay in the zone he had created. Softly and tenderly, Jamie ministered to Grant, who stood still for him. Grabbing another towel, Jamie quickly dried himself then led Grant into the bedroom.

"I don't know about you, but one touch and I'm going to be gone. I'm serious, Jamie. Just a touch of your hand, and it's all over." Grant was about to lose it just looking at his lover as Jamie pulled him onto the bed.

"Come here, baby. It doesn't matter what we do. You know that."

Grant crawled up and lay right on top of Jamie, lining them up perfectly. Jamie's arms came around him, and he began to grind his hips into Jamie's. Both of them were leaking just enough to make it a smooth rub. Within just a few minutes, they were both coming and gasping. Grant dropped his head to Jamie's neck and breathed in deeply.

"I love you. I'm sorry that wasn't—"

"Don't you even think it. You know anything we do together is right. If I'm not mistaken, we came at the same time. What's better than that? Proves we were right together. It doesn't have to be full-out sex all the time. I'm tired, you're tired, and we're so close. I'm happy just being with you at last. You're right, it seems like forever since we were like this. Was it just this morning?" Jamie moved his hands over Grant's head and back as he talked.

"Yeah, I'm okay when we're like this. Let's clean up and get some sleep. We're getting up really early tomorrow and going shopping." Grant nuzzled his face deeper into Jamie's neck, loving the smell and the comfort that spot always brought him.

Jamie reached over to the table for a towel and wiped them both clean, dropping it to the side of the trashcan when he was done. He drew Grant back into his arms, and Grant snuggled into his side, sighing heavily.

"We'll get through this, and we'll be stronger for it. Don't let it get you down, Grant. We're meant to be together. I really believe that. No one could be better for me. I love you."

"I love you, too. I'm not letting anything or anyone come between us. We're in this together. Kiss now and then the cuddle rule still applies here, ya know?"

Jamie laughed and kissed Grant. Grant smiled as they lay quietly with arms around each other, his head on Jamie's shoulder as the cuddle after sex rule was enforced.

Chapter Nine

Monday and Tuesday passed with no new developments, but Grant could not relax. He worried about Jamie working here every day with some idiot trying to hurt him. As promised, Jamie had asked if any of Jim's crew would like extra work. One of the men had been off because of an accident. He'd healed and was just waiting for the doctor's okay to go back to full time work. Adam was his name, and Grant would meet him tonight at the cookout.

Last night, he and Jamie had put some chicken breasts in to marinate, and Jamie was already home when Grant pulled in. They had about an hour before everyone was showing up. Since it was a work night, they had to start it late, but being summer it would be light for a couple of hours. Grant was going to make a big pan of baked beans and some ramen noodle slaw. Boy, did Jamie love that stuff! Who knew something so simple would make the man so happy?

He'd wait until just before they ate to finish that. Right now, he came in the back door to find Jamie readying the items he'd need to grill the meat.

"Hey, honey, I'm home."

"How was your day, dear?" Jamie turned to him, depositing the lettuce and tomatoes onto the counter to open his arms. Oh, yeah, his day just got better.

"Call all those people and tell them we're cancelling. I want you for supper," Grant said, the last words right onto Jamie's lips. The end of the word supper made just the perfect pucker. Jamie slipped right in and took advantage of the opening Grant provided. Grant's tongue came out to play with Jamie's, and he didn't hesitate to wrap his arms around Jamie's neck. He finally broke the kiss with little nibbles along Jamie's lips, followed by smacking his mouth.

"Nothing on the menu could beat that. Just no offering it up to anyone else," Grant teased.

"Like I would," Jamie answered.

"Hey, where's Brit? He usually comes running."

"He's in his corner, being punished, so no petting him until I call him out." Jamie looked stern.

"What in the world did he do?" Grant couldn't imagine Brit doing anything that would warrant punishment.

"Dug up a good portion of the flowerbed," Jamie said.

"No way. Jamie, that is *so* not like Brit. What the hell?" Grant just looked at Jamie, scenarios running through his head. "Are you sure there wasn't a good reason? Like did freak person do something to the flowers?" Grant was trying to give Brit every benefit of the doubt.

"I don't know. I came home, let him out and he went straight for the flowers and started barking and growling and digging them up. Since it wasn't the usual place he gets upset about, I tried to get him to quit. I went back there, but it was just flowers, *now* a mess of them." Jamie looked confused about the whole deal. He clearly hated punishing Brit but hadn't known what to do.

"Let's go look closer. We can take a few minutes. And…I think we should take him with us, okay?" Grant wanted to see Brit at the scene.

"Okay. Brit, come here, boy." Nails skidded on the floor as Brit joined them, eager to be back in their good graces. No doubt he didn't understand being punished in the first place.

When Jamie opened the door, Brit shot off the patio and headed straight for the flowers, though he did stop dead when he reached them. Jamie and Grant walked out and stood by him, looking at the mess. Brit took a tentative step forward and sniffed then looked up at them as if to say, "Smell that?"

Grant looked at Jamie and said, "After you." He pointed to the ground, and Jamie grinned at him like it was a challenge. Grant knelt with him and there they were on hands and knees by the flower garden. He hoped no one showed up early.

"So, what am I doing down here?" Jamie said, looking from Brit to Grant.

"I don't know, but you know Brit's not destructive, so make like a dog and sniff." Grant said, bending down and taking a whiff.

"Aw, damn!"

"What?" Jamie said at Grant's explosion.

"No, you smell then tell me." Grant wanted to see if he was right before he lost it completely. He watched as Jamie bent and took a big sniff and jerked back with horror in his face.

"That motherfucker pissed on our flowers!" Then Jamie realised what he had done and turned a contrite face to Brit. "Brit, I'm so sorry. I should've known better. Come here, boy. Yeah, I'm sorry." Jamie was hugging Brit, and Grant could hear the sincerity in his voice. Brit took it like the trooper he was, accepting the apology and giving love as usual. Jamie and Brit were having their make-up moment, and Grant looked on, smiling as they wrestled and played together.

To Jamie, Brit was a member of the family. They'd talked about how he understood what they were saying, not just the usual commands used for dogs. Brit was special. Grant figured Jamie felt like he'd hurt Brit's feelings when he punished him for something he should have praised him for — bringing their attention to the fact that the intruder had been there again. Peeing on their flowers wasn't as bad as putting a rattler on the patio, but it just showed the man was cocky and a real bastard.

"Well, we don't have time to clean up the mess now, and we can tell Wade and Mark when they come by later. Come on, let's go in. I've got to clean up and I'll help with supper. God, it's something every day with this guy."

Jamie got up, and they headed back in. Grant put his arm around Jamie and said, "I can't believe Wade couldn't find out anything about Donnie. What could that mean, Jamie?"

"I don't know. I mean, he said the person he talked to at the prison told him that Donnie had been transferred. So that means we have no way of knowing when he gets out. He shouldn't be out yet, but if he's not there, and we have no idea where he is, how are we going to — shit! It's all fucked up, Grant. I don't even want to think of that nutwad being out of prison and messing with us again."

"Do we have any rights about finding out where he is or when he gets out? I mean, as the victims in the case last year, don't we have some kind of rights?" Grant asked. He hated to admit that this hadn't occurred to him back then. They should have checked out what they could do about getting information about Donnie's release. Surely to God, Donnie was not out of prison and dogging them.

"I don't know, baby. We'll ask Wade who we should talk to in order to find out what recourse we do have. Maybe none. I've heard that a lot of times, the victims don't have as many rights as the criminals. We'll see."

They went in and got busy on the planned event ahead. A couple of hours later, they were all on the patio, and they'd pulled up the picnic table from back in the yard to seat everyone closer together. Grant had doubled the recipe for the slaw Jamie loved so much, and it was completely gone. He'd had to promise the recipe to several people already.

When Wade and Mark showed up, there were a lot of jokes about who was getting busted and why, but it died down when explanations were made. Questions flew back and forth as Jamie and Grant tried to keep up with telling them what had been done when and so on. The main group gathered to talk while Jamie and Grant pulled the officers out into the yard by the garden and told them the latest.

Wade promised to write it up and told them he was still trying to find out more about where Donnie actually was now. He sounded put out that as a fellow law officer he was being given the run-around about Donnie's whereabouts.

"I'll look into who you should talk to about your rights. I know there's a form that people can fill out that gives them the right to call the prison for information. But it has to have already been on file. Just anybody can't call and get info on an inmate. Heaven forbid that we invade their civil rights."

They walked back to the group and Grant went to fix them a couple of plates. He apologised for the lack of slaw and laughed when everyone talked about how good it was. The look on Wade's face was priceless.

"I promise to make some for you when we cook out again. It's really easy. Come on, sit down and eat. I know you have to go back to work. Thanks for coming by. Enjoy your meal while I go get the dessert ready."

There were suddenly lots of voices and interest in what was going on.

"What's for dessert?"

"Is there cake?"

"Is it brownies?"

"Mmm, I don't care, just get me something sweet."

"Need any help?"

He hurried inside to get away from all the silliness. He knew dessert would be a hit. He'd made a big trifle and put it in a punch bowl that he'd gotten at a discount store. It looked fancy and very chi-chi. It was just broken up pieces of angel food cake, vanilla pudding, strawberry Jello and Cool Whip mixed together, and sliced strawberries layered over and over and covered on the top with toasted slivered almonds.

He yelled for Jamie to come help him carry it out. He just needed assistance with the paper bowls, napkins, and forks that he'd put into a basket. He was certainly gratified with the 'Oohs' and 'Ahs' he received when he carried it out to the table. With a big spoon, he doled out servings and was again pleased when there was near silence broken by the occasional 'Mmm' sound.

Jamie reached over and squeezed his thigh and said, "Good job, baby."

While he cleaned up, with Mark's help, Jamie made plans to start on the framing of the patio the next day. They would screen it in with a door on the left side where the steps were and another in the back where the steps went down into the yard — the patio was about four feet off the ground with four steps down. When all the construction was done, the deck would be at the bottom of those four steps.

While Grant and Mark did the dishes and cleaned up things in the kitchen, Grant could hear the conversation outside. He wasn't paying too much attention until Jamie mentioned the camera they were planning to install while they were working. He shivered as he thought of what they might catch on film this time.

Grant looked forward to the screened in porch and Jamie was especially looking forward to the hot tub and grill being out on the deck. Grant loved that they both enjoyed being outdoors and this would make that even more special.

Grant was anxious now for everyone to leave since he had planned a surprise for Jamie tonight. Jamie was high because he was taking a vacation for the first time in a long time and was excited about the construction job. Grant wanted him to remember tonight for a while. The cookout had been fun, and they'd gotten a lot of planning done, but soon it was going to be just the two of them. While Jamie was making last minute plans with Adam and Jim and a couple of others who would be here tomorrow for the first part of the project, Grant was setting the stage for the next part of the night.

He'd always loved a song by Leonard Cohen. The man's gravelly voice as he slowly listed all the reasons why he was 'your man'...well, Grant knew Jamie would get a kick out of it. He had candles ready to light and some nice Bailey's chilled and set up in a bucket on the bedside table. He was going to ask Jamie to just listen as he went along with the words to the song, telling him that he was in fact, Jamie's man.

"Hey, everything's locked up. Where'd you get to? Oh, my...look at this. You got something on your mind there? I like it," Jamie said, eyes roving from the candles Grant lit to the bucket and glasses to the towel by the bed. There was nothing slow about Jamie. He went right to the Bailey's and poured each of them just a little bit into the glasses. Grant turned on the CD with the song lined up.

When the music started, Jamie's eyebrows raised comically, and he grinned.

"What is that? I've never heard that before? Oh, wow, what a sexy voice..."

"Just listen to the words, okay?" Grant asked, and since the song was so slow, he sang along with it. It was almost like talking so he wasn't embarrassed at his singing voice.

He was essentially telling Jamie that whatever he needed, whatever he wanted, Grant was his man, up to the task, ready to do whatever. The song was perfect for what he wanted to convey. The lyrics stated that 'if you want a partner take my hand' and later 'if you wanted a boxer I'd step into the ring' and 'if you wanted to play doctor then I'd examine every inch of you' and still later 'if you've got to sleep on the road I'll steer for you'. It was exactly how Grant felt about Jamie. Anything he needed or wanted, Grant would be that or do that for him.

There was no doubt that Jamie loved the way Grant sang it to him. Grant was playing it up just a little, with the occasional swing of his hips and bat of his lashes to show Jamie that while he was trying to entertain him, he was also saying something special to him. Grant could tell that Jamie got it. Jamie never took his eyes off Grant, and more than once, he reached for him, but Grant stayed back until the song ended. As the last notes died, Grant turned the CD player off, and when he moved to turn back to Jamie, he found himself caught. Kind of what he was hoping for, to tell the truth.

"That was the coolest thing ever. Where'd you get that neat song? I love it. No, I love that *you* sang it to me. Sexy man, Grant, you are one sexy, hot man. I thank God every day that you're mine. Come here, have a nice drink then I think I'd like to play doctor and have you examine me all over. Then it'll be my turn."

"Certainly, doctor. Where would you like me?" Grant asked, his lips not far from Jamie's.

Jamie laughed and closed that space, kissing him with a fervour that was broken up by chuckles as he tried to move Grant to the bed.

"What's so funny?" Grant asked, as they stopped by the table with the glasses on it.

"The idea that what I have planned for you could happen in a doctor's office. Not in this lifetime, baby. Here, want a sip? You make me so happy," Jamie stated, handing Grant one of the glasses.

Instead of picking his up, Jamie leaned in and stole a taste from Grant's mouth. Grant shared happily. Getting into the game, he pulled back and took another sip, keeping this one in his mouth and going back to Jamie. This time the cool, sweet liquor was distributed between the two hungry mouths. Tongues played and little by little the liquid disappeared, and only passion remained to keep them joined.

"Yum, that never tasted so good. Role play over. I just want my Grant."

"Take me." Grant stepped back an inch or so and put his arms out, presenting Jamie with himself, like a gift. The look in Jamie's eyes as he looked Grant up and down was enough to have him eager to be taken. That was just fine with Grant. He'd gotten the night started, and he'd be fine with Jamie taking over and getting just what he wanted.

Grant stood and let Jamie undress him, turning or bending as indicated. He'd already disposed of his shoes and socks so it wasn't long before he stood before Jamie, naked and wanting.

When Grant had still been recovering from the many injuries caused by his traffic accident last year, Jamie had been inventive in his lovemaking in an effort to not cause Grant any harm. Some of those positions and techniques remained favourites. Grant loved being bent over the side of their tall bed and taken from behind. Before, it was done to protect his healing knee. Since then, they both had come to enjoy this particular form of sex.

While he loved sex with Jamie face-to-face due to the intimacy and emotion of being able to look into his eyes, there was something so primal about the feeling of being taken like this from behind. Loving Jamie as he did just made the intensity stronger. It was all about sensation and excitement.

Jamie had stripped in record time, and Grant nearly groaned as Jamie kissed him and turned him to face the bed. Grant didn't need encouragement. He bent and placed his chest on the bed, stepping up so that his behind was presented to Jamie. Hearing Jamie open the lube and put on the condom had Grant squirming in anticipation. He moved his ass, knowing Jamie would love it.

"Getting impatient, love? I'm here." Jamie stood behind Grant, his legs nudging right against Grant's. He bent and Grant was completely enclosed in Jamie's arms. Jamie spread a line of fire down the centre of Grant's back, alternating nips and licks, sucks and kisses.

Grant moved his hips, bumping into Jamie's groin, feeling Jamie's hard cock, right...just almost there! Yes! Mmm, please...

Jamie didn't waste any more time, and Grant groaned as he felt slick fingers breaching his hole and sliding into him. He relaxed into the bed and let Jamie have his way. Lightning bolts of sensation woke depths of passion in him as Jamie twisted and turned his fingers, finding Grant's prostate and teasing it until he couldn't be still.

"Jamie!" He didn't have to say more. Jamie knew what he needed and soon Grant felt Jamie's cock pushing into him, stretching and causing more zings of pleasure to spread throughout his body from the area that Jamie was working so hard. Jamie's hands grasped Grant's hips and held him steady for the thrusts that followed. Grant pushed back into Jamie's forward movements and couldn't help the groans that burst from him.

God, he'd needed this, needed Jamie and this intense connection with him. He squeezed his muscles against Jamie, giving him as much return pleasure as he could. Grant's cock was being rhythmically crushed against the sheet where he'd turned back the bed earlier. Just a couple more times and he'd be coming all over Jamie's side of the bed.

"Jamie," he gasped. "Towel." Grant felt the towel hit the back of his hand. He grabbed it and pushed it under him, cupping his cock and moving his hand up and down twice before he came, hard, into the terrycloth glove. Shuddering and gasping, he felt his muscles tightening on Jamie's cock as Jamie filled the condom with cum and the air with his shouts of completion.

"Grant! Love you. God, baby, I love you. Hold on, let me just, yeah, careful." Grant felt him ease out.

Grant lay there for a second, recovering his breath and waiting for Jamie to return from the bathroom. He knew what would come next. They always took care of each other. Ah, there. A warm washcloth was smoothed over his ass, between his cheeks, cleaning him. Jamie pulled him up and took the soiled towel from him. Folding the washcloth, he swiped it over Grant's cock and abdomen. Holding the linens in his hand, with the other Jamie held the back of Grant's neck as he took a swift kiss, before stepping away for a moment.

In seconds, Jamie was back from the bathroom again. Grant still stood by the bed, just waiting. Jamie walked right into him, full body contact, and wrapped Grant right up in his arms.

"Hey baby. Do you know how much I love you? I know I tell you, but I'm not sure I can make you understand how much, how deeply I feel about you. I never want to be without you." Jamie ended his impassioned speech by taking Grant's mouth in a long sweet kiss. He took his time, nibbling on Grant's lips, teasing the corners with his tongue. Grant shivered and pressed into Jamie's mouth, wanting more of the tender treatment.

Grant thrilled to the fact that he and Jamie were so alike. They loved having sex, making love, expressing their desire in countless and varied ways. He figured that not all men enjoyed the tenderness that they both indulged in so happily. Neither fell for the belief that you had to be macho and rough to be a real man. Grant and Jamie were both strong, tough men, but they felt being gentle and caring did not emasculate them, it strengthened them.

Grant knew he'd hit the gold mine with Jamie and that's where his meaning of life came from. The life they were making together was everything to Grant. He liked his job, he worked and played well with others, but his joy and happiness came from his living and loving with Jamie Taylor. Sometimes, his great fortune brought tears to his eyes. Just his luck, Jamie pulled back as his thoughts were reaching that point.

"Baby? Are you all right? What is it?" Jamie kissed each cheek right below his eyes, tracing across the top of his nose to do so, making him smile.

"I'm fine, Jamie. I'm just thinking about how much I love you and how lucky we are to be together."

"That's it?" Jamie asked, reaching up to take the band from Grant's hair, running his hand up the back of Grant's head, through the loose strands.

"Mostly, I was also thinking about how I love the way we are with each other. That's all, just the way we love, Jamie."

"Ah, yes, the way we love, Grant. That's everything, isn't it?"

"Yeah. It is. Come on, let's go to bed. Tomorrow, you become my sexy construction worker guy. Fantasy time. I can't wait to come home and find you all sweaty and dusty, with a tool belt around your waist," Grant told him, crawling onto the bed and holding his arms out to Jamie.

"Sounds like you've been thinking about this, huh? I'll try to make that fantasy come true for you. I have a feeling tomorrow night might be exciting for me," Jamie teased, sliding right into Grant's open arms.

"There's a strong possibility," Grant admitted, chuckling as Jamie settled against him, and they both sighed, tired and happy, fear forgotten for the night.

* * * *

Meanwhile, Donnie decided that it was times to step things up. He'd gotten a real chuckle out of Jamie's anger over the flowers. Pussy! When Jamie had yelled at that damn dog, Donnie had loved it.

He had to be really careful and really quiet as he performed the next trick in his bag. Oh, he was like a magician, with a world of ideas for ways to freak out the pervy boys. He'd completely forgotten that once he'd been sexually interested in Jamie. Prison had turned that into a deep and lasting hate for anyone and anything that had to do with...*that*.

He moved slowly and carefully, listening for that fuckin' dog. This was going to be good. He wished he could watch this one. The setup took almost an hour, but he was pleased with the result. He didn't care if it was Jamie or Grant as long as it got one of them. While he was at it, he decided to go ahead and throw in another little head puzzler.

Yep, this was a good night.

Chapter Ten

Grant wiped the sweat from his forehead again and wished one more time that he had one of those terry bands that soaked it up before it ran into his eyes. Despite the fact that he was assistant to the assistant, who was about to retire, he still did a lot of the down and dirty work. Today, he was working with the maintenance crew. There was a lot of mowing and landscaping work to be done, and two of the workers were out—one whose wife was delivering their first child and the other had cut his arm and was off for the week. Grant filled in.

He really didn't mind the work, since he was out in the sun and air all day. But it was almost July and hot as hell. Stopping the big mower, he bent to grab his water bottle and drank, wishing he could take his bill cap off and pour it over his head. It was times like this that he wished his hair was as short as Jamie's. But then he thought about Jamie's hands in it, and that thought went away. Now that the mower was idling, the world seemed weirdly silent under the big headphones.

Glancing at the field, he figured he had about another half hour or forty-five minutes before he'd be done and headed back to the office. It was almost two o'clock and really too hot to be doing this. As it was, he'd stop at the pool and use the shower there before going back to the main building. Being prepared for just such a situation, he had a change of clothes in the truck.

He put the bottle back and started the mower again, lost in thoughts of how Jamie and the crew at home were doing. He pictured Jamie in tight jeans and T-shirt and that heavy belt hanging low on his hips.

He went round and round the field, mind happily occupied with thoughts not anywhere near the work at hand.

As he made a turn he saw one of the park vehicles coming full speed across the field towards him. What the hell? He stopped the mower and got off. The driver skidded to a stop near him, and his first thought was that something had happened to the assistant and he was needed back at the building. He drew the headphones off and started for the truck. Ah, it was Matt.

"Grant, come on. It's your man. It's Jamie."

"What? What are you... What's Jamie? Matt, what's Jamie?" Grant's heart stopped, and he felt the blood draining from his face. Was he going to faint? What was going on? He took a deep breath and grabbed the window frame.

"Are you okay, man? Uh, you look, like, really bad." Matt was wasting time.

"Matt! Focus! What's Jamie? Why are you here? Tell me!" Grant slapped the side of the truck. Now his heart was racing, pounding, hurting. Fear gripped him.

"Tony sent me. You've got to go. Jamie's hurt. Go to the hospital. Get in. I'm to take you to your truck so you can go straight there. He's at the Med Centre." Matt motioned for him to get in the truck, and in seconds, he was spitting up dust and grass as he flew back across the field.

Why hadn't someone called him on his cell? He reached into his pocket and pulled it out. Shit! Five messages. He hadn't been able to hear it or feel it vibrate since he was on the mower with the headphones on. He started running through them, his hand bouncing in front of his face as they raced towards the parking lot.

Jamie hurt. Med Centre. Hurry.
Jamie needs you.
Med Centre. Emrgcy room.
Grant? Jamie hurt bad.
Grant, where are u?

Jesus! His knees bounced, he wrung his hands, and he was sure his heart would be damaged somehow when this was all said and done. It couldn't keep on beating this hard and not just explode. He began to shake all over. Finally, they reached his truck. Tony stood beside it. Grant almost fell out of Matt's truck.

Tony grabbed Grant's arm and drew him to the passenger side of his own truck.

"Give me the keys. Get in. Matt, tell Barker I'll call from the hospital and let him know if I'll be back today or not. He knows what to do. After that, why don't you finish what Grant was doing then report to Barker to see what he wants you to do next."

"Yes, sir. Uh, good luck, Grant, with your guy." Matt was a young college student, majoring in Recreation and

Parks Administration. He was doing a good job for them and was a nice young man. He seemed to be all right with Grant and Jamie, too. Another plus in the man's favour.

In just a few more seconds, Tony was pulling out onto the road and heading for the hospital.

"Do you know what happened? Tony, tell me if you know anything."

"All I know is something happened at the house while they were working out back. Something about his leg and a lot of blood. Sorry, I'm sorry. That's all they said. They were kind of frantic. Don't think the worst, okay? Let's just hold on until we get there."

Tony meant well, but his words weren't helping Grant's unstoppable shaking. He hoped he could walk in when they got there. *Please God, don't let him be hurt that bad. Don't let me lose him. I can't lose him. I can't...*

"You're not going to lose him. Come on, Grant. Suck it up. He's going to need you to be strong no matter what it is. Fall apart later, okay. I'll help you, but don't you let him down." Tony's tough love did the trick.

Hell no, he wasn't going to let Jamie down. He sat up straight as they turned in at the emergency department of the hospital. Tony drew up under the portico and let Grant out.

"Go on, find him. I'll be right in." Tony was a good friend.

Grant sprinted in, hitting the doors and bursting into the area, head turning both ways like he was going to just find Jamie sitting there waiting for him. He saw a desk and hurried over.

"Jamie Taylor. I need to see him. We're...we're partners. We live together. Please, I have to know if he's all right."

"Are you next of kin?"

"Yes." Grant was no fool.

She wasn't either, looking at him over the top of her glasses. He held his breath, getting ready to argue, bitch, scream, have a tantrum—whatever it took. Bless the gods, she winked at him and said, "He's in room four, down the hall on the left. Relax, honey, he's going to live."

Grant didn't wait for more. He was at the door to room four almost before she got the last words out of her mouth. He paused a moment and took a deep breath and pushed open the door, peeking in to see if there was going to be a problem with him going in.

Blood everywhere. There was blood *everywhere*. What were they doing to him? There was a nurse on the opposite side of the bed doing something to his arm and another sitting on a stool dropping a bloody bandage onto the floor with what looked like a hundred other bloody ones. Jamie was pale and had his eyes closed. He looked as if he were in a lot of pain. But he was alive. Grant nearly sobbed with relief.

"Jamie?" Grant spoke softly, hesitantly.

Jamie turned his head to the door and those eyes, those pretty blue eyes, opened. He raised his hand to Grant and curled his finger in a 'come here' gesture. Grant stepped over to him quickly. He gasped as he got close enough to see Jamie's left leg.

"Jesus, what *happened*? Is he okay?" Grant looked at the nurse who was working on Jamie's leg. It bled from ankle to halfway up his thigh on the outside. Obviously they were having a hard time getting the bleeding to stop. The nurse glanced up at him quickly then back to what she was doing, which looked to be pressing bandage after bandage on his leg, bearing down, wiping off, and getting another and starting it again.

"Baby?" Grant hated the way his voice sounded, teary and scared. "What happened? Can you tell me? Can I do something?"

"You're here. That's all I need." Jamie held tightly to Grant's hand and squeezed every time the nurse pressed hard.

She began to speak. "I'm Doctor Young. I'm glad you're here. You must be his Grant. He's been desperate to see you. It seems he fell through some boards and scraped his leg, all the way up. It's pretty deep in a couple of places. He says he tried to move away when he felt the board giving way but wasn't fast enough and went through. I don't think anything is broken, and if we're lucky, he won't even need stitches. But he's going to hurt for a few days, and it'll be stiff for a while."

Grant looked from her to Jamie, swallowing hard to keep the bile down. Jamie was going to be all right. It wasn't going to be fun, but Jamie was okay. It was all he could do not to bend down and kiss Jamie and hide his face in that neck. He put his other hand on Jamie's face, stroking across his forehead and down his cheek. God, this was probably the first good breath he'd taken in the last half hour or so.

"We were working, had the front section of the patio, next to the house, framed and were getting ready to do the back part. A good portion of the morning was spent going through materials and marking things and so on. I stepped on the back edge on the left side and it just broke. I went straight down, Grant. I tried to throw myself forward so I'd end up in the yard, but it happened so fast. If I hadn't done that, I'd probably be raw on both sides of my leg. It hurts, Grant. Really hurts."

"Mr. Taylor, that's probably because there are a vast number of splinters all the way up your leg. Now that we're getting the bleeding slowed down, we're going to have to take those out. I wouldn't doubt that you'll find some buried and working their way out for days. With the way the wood was broken so roughly, it left lots of pieces behind." She motioned to the nurse who came and cleared away the stack of bloody dressings, making Grant feel better immediately. Seeing that much of Jamie's blood was almost more than he could take.

Doctor Young went on, "I'll get all of them out that I can and clean it well, both of which will be fairly painful. I'm sorry about that. I'll give you something for the pain and something for the next few days. You don't want to let it get stiff. As it scabs, you'll have to moisten it with lotion and oil, which I'll prescribe, so it can be bent and moved without breaking open the wounds until they begin to heal."

"I'll take care of him. Is there anything he should do or that I can do? He's on vacation this week and all next week. Does he need to stay off it?" Grant wanted to know exactly what Jamie could do because he knew Jamie would fight it and want to get back to helping. Knowing what the doctor said would help Grant argue the point if need be.

"His pain will dictate what he can do. I don't want the wounds broken open, but if they're kept soft and allowed to heal, he should be fine in a few weeks. He'll be up and about in a couple of days, but don't let him do too much. Looks like you might have some influence here, huh?" She smiled at the two of them. Grant's hand was still on Jamie, having slid down to rest on his shoulder now and the other was still grasped tightly in Jamie's. Grant felt it every time they pulled out another splinter.

So, he went ahead and talked about the elephant in the room.

"Was it an accident, or was it another one for the police?"

Before Jamie could answer, Tony was at the door and Jim was right behind him, a piece of wood in his hand.

"Grant, could you come here a minute? Hey, Jamie. Glad you're okay. Be back in a minute." With those words, Tony stepped back into the hall and waited for Grant to join him. Grant squeezed Jamie's hand and turned to the door. What now? He was afraid he knew. Why else would they bring a piece of the wood with them?

"Okay, tell me straight out."

"It's been sawed through, almost all the way. It wouldn't have mattered who stepped on it, they were going to go through. I've called the police and asked for that guy that you all know. Johnson, isn't it? He's on his way here. Jim will stay here. I've called and Matt is coming to pick me up. I'm glad Jamie isn't hurt worse. God knows this is bad enough. He bled a lot and scared them all pretty bad. I'm so sorry."

"Hey, it's okay. You go on back. I don't know when I can get back. I'll try..."

"You take the rest of today and tomorrow, no take the rest of the week off. We'd already arranged for Friday, anyway. If he's better by Monday, come back then. We'll manage. Life happens and you deal with it. Hang in there. I'm glad he's got you." Tony stepped around Grant and went in to say a few words to Jamie.

Tony left, but before Grant could go back in, Officers Johnson and Thomas were hurrying down the hall. Damn it, he wanted to get back to Jamie. He needed to get back to Jamie.

"Come on in here, you all. Jamie needs to hear this, and I don't want to leave him alone anymore. I need to be in there. Wade, you're going to love this one." Grant knew his voice was full of sarcasm, but he was well past tired of this shit. Jamie could have torn open an artery and bled to death right in the backyard. What if—

Don't go there!

"Hey guys," Jamie said. "Oh, what did you find, Jim? Evidently it isn't good if our friends are here. Doctor Young, this is Officer Johnson and Officer Thomas. They're working on our case. The other guy is Jim Hook. He was working on the patio with me. It seems someone is trying to play tricks on us or hurt us or kill us. We're not sure which, or even why. Officers, Doctor Young." Jamie made the introductions as if they were at a party instead of around his bed where he was being de-splintered. The grimace on his face gave testament to how badly that hurt.

Grant went right back and took his hand.

Jim held out the piece of thick wood to the officers. It was easy to see that three fourths of the edge was smooth and about a fourth of it was jagged. Someone had sawed almost all the way through it. Grant was filled with rage as he watched the officers, their friends, study it and start writing in their tablets.

"This has to stop. It's getting more and more dangerous. I don't want to live like this again. Scared all the time." Grant threw the words out there. Useless words. Redundant words. What use were they? They all knew those facts.

Wade spoke up in full police manner, flipping his tablet closed. "We'll take this in and write it up. Doctor Young,

I'd like to get a copy of the report on this, if I can. This is part of a criminal investigation." He turned to Grant and Jamie and said, "I'll see you all later when I find out more. Take care of each other."

After the officers left, Grant turned back Doctor Young with a question.

"He can come home today, right? I can take him home when you're finished with, uh, what you're doing?" Grant was losing all feeling in his hand as Jamie continued to grasp it tightly, squeezing hard each time she pulled another splinter out of his tortured flesh. Some were larger than others, but all of them seemed to be causing a lot of pain. Poor Jamie!

"Yes, he'll be fine to go as soon as I finish this and clean it thoroughly. I'll put a dressing on it and let you know when to change it and how to go about it safely. He'll need antibiotics and the medicine for pain." She stopped as Jamie jerked on the table. "Be still, Mr. Taylor. I'm almost done here."

When it was all said and done, Jamie needed six stitches in one spot below his knee. By the time they left, Grant knew his hand would be bruised and sore, but it was little compared to what Jamie was going through. Grant helped Jamie into the truck, after scooting the seat back as far as it would go so Jamie could stretch his leg out.

Grant drove slowly, trying to avoid bumps and potholes. He knew that every movement caused pain in Jamie's legs. Sweat broke out on Jamie's brow as they made their way through traffic and headed home. Grant kept an eye on Jamie but left him alone. Jamie's head was back on the headrest, eyes closed, lips clenched.

As they pulled into the driveway, Grant was pleased to see Jim and another couple of guys come through the gate from the back of the house. He'd already planned to take Jamie in the front door, since it was easier to navigate. Jim opened Jamie's door, and Grant came around to help him ease out of the truck, while keeping his leg straight. Grant put Jamie's left arm over his shoulder, making sure not to bump his leg. Handing the house keys to Jim, they headed to the front door. Jamie was a little shaky though mobile. They stood, waiting for Jim to unlock the door. Jamie looked down and made a noise that Grant was surprised he could hear over the excited barking they heard from inside the house.

"Hey." Jamie's voice was a little slurred, while he stood there most of his weight on his right leg and his arm tight around Grant's shoulders. "Look down there, Grant. Um, how did we miss that? Has it been there since last year? It's not blood. It's not the right colour. I thought we got it all the paint cleaned up. Hmm..."

"Jamie, hon? What are you talking about?" Grant looked down and saw that Jamie was pointing to what looked like three drops of red paint. One drop was larger and the other two were very small. The paint was directly in front of the door and was bright red. Granted, they used the back door a lot, but it's wasn't as if they never used the front door. He found it hard to believe that they would have missed seeing these drops of paint for a whole year.

"What in the world? I don't think that's been there this whole year, Jamie. We would have seen it. Come on, let's get you inside. We'll figure that out later." Grant made a mental note to tell Wade. "You want the couch or the bed? I'm thinking you might need the bed for a little while. You're a little loopy, and I know you're in pain."

"Jim, can you make sure Brit doesn't jump on Jamie just yet. We'll need to make sure he knows where he can't touch." Grant turned to Jim as they stepped in past him. "Thanks for staying here and for your help earlier." Jim took hold of Brit's collar and tried to calm him until the two men got inside.

"No problem. The police came by and looked at the whole scene and told us we could continue if we wanted. We all decided to keep working. We got the main frame up and one of the guys will help me the next couple of days so we won't get too far behind. I'm really sorry this happened. I, uh, I hosed away all the blood and cleaned the place up. We'll be here for about two more hours and back early tomorrow. Take it easy, Jamie. We've got your back."

God, friends are wonderful things.

"Brit! Hi, buddy. Hey, easy now. I'm okay. It's okay, I promise. Calm down now," Jamie said as he held onto Brit's head and petted him, keeping him in front of his body. Grant still had hold of Jamie, making sure he didn't just topple over. Soon, Brit calmed down and followed them through the room, staying on Jamie's right side. He knew. Of course, he knew how to act around someone who was injured.

Jim and the guys were soon working and hammering out back, and Grant got Jamie to the bathroom, and they stood a minute looking at the bed. Jamie looked at him, seeming confused.

"What's the matter?" Grant had hold of Jamie's arm to steady him.

"We're going to have to switch sides. I need you to, I mean, I need to…"

It hadn't been hard to figure out what Jamie needed. "I get it. Come on over here and you can get in on my side. That way I can hold you without touching that leg."

"Thank you. I need you to stay with me, hold me, just for a little. I don't want to think about what happened. It was deliberate. I know that, but right now, I'm so tired and I hurt and I just want to lie down with you. Can we do that?" Jamie had never seemed so depressed, so down, ever. Of course, he was in pain and on medication for it. There might also be a little bit of adrenaline let down after the traumatic last few hours.

"Of course. Here, let me help you get these shorts off. You stand still and I'll make sure they don't touch that part of your leg. Good, now then your shirt. Hey, can you stand still just a second?"

"Sure, maybe, I think. Why? What are you doing?" Jamie looked at him, head tilted, with an adorable confused look on his face. Brit still stood right beside Jamie, nudging his right leg, letting him know he was there for him, but still and quiet now.

"I'll be right back." Grant could smack himself for not thinking of this while he was in the bathroom, but he knew he could make Jamie feel just a little better. Quickly, he grabbed a hand towel and got it wet, wringing it out and hurrying back to Jamie. He stood in front of Jamie and smoothed the cloth over Jamie's face and neck. Jamie's sigh was just what Grant needed. He knew his Jamie. Swiping the towel over Jamie's shoulders and back, down his arms, he held on to Jamie. Dropping the towel onto the side of the trashcan by the bedside table, he turned back around to help Jamie ease onto the bed.

Grant walked around to what was usually Jamie's side and crawled up and over beside Jamie.

"Come here, love. How about you just rest on me for a while and take a nap. We'll talk later, I promise. We both need this right now. Sleep now. I won't let you go."

Jamie turned, put his head on Grant's shoulder and moved so that his poor mangled leg was resting as comfortably as possible and in seconds was sound asleep. Grant leaned to put a gentle kiss on Jamie's forehead. He looked over to where Brit was sitting by his bed in the corner. "Rest Brit. I've got him. It's okay now." Brit settled on the floor.

It was over. *Sort of.* They were home and safe and in each other's arms. That was the best thing ever. Grant didn't think he'd ever been so scared. Well, maybe a couple of times last year, but they'd thought that mess was all finished. Grant just wasn't ready to go through all this terror crap again. Nothing could happen to Jamie. He couldn't bear it, he thought as he tightened his arms around Jamie and turned a little more into him.

Grant didn't sleep. He held Jamie for two hours while Jamie slept hard, gasping or groaning every time he moved accidently and caused himself pain. Grant soothed him each time with strokes and murmurs. He got up when he heard a light knock at the back door. Checking his watch he figured it was Jim and the guys leaving for the day. Easing away from Jamie, he slipped out, closing the door.

Grant thanked them again for what they'd done for Jamie, for continuing the work, and for coming back tomorrow. He told them he would provide lunch for the next few days since he would be here with Jamie. They invited him out to see what they'd gotten done. Grant's eyes immediately went to the left side of the back of the patio. The frame that they'd gotten done covered the place where Jamie had gone through.

"We bought a new board and replaced it. Now the frame is there so it's all good. We'll work on the screening and the doors tomorrow. We'll get that camera put up, too. We know where Jamie wants it. After that, we can start on the lower deck. You take care of Jamie. We'll get this done for y'all."

Jim was a nice man. They were making friends right and left. It looked as if they were going to need all of them.

After the men left, Grant went in to make some supper. Jamie would wake soon and needed some good food. Despite it being hot as hell outside, Grant put together a hearty vegetable-beef soup. He had it bubbling and smelling wonderful in short order. Jamie loved his soup and right now he needed comfort food.

Looking through the cabinets, he tried to find something to make for dessert, something Jamie would like. Seeing a couple of bags of oyster crackers, he grabbed them and took out two cookie sheets. They both loved the crackers seasoned with garlic salt, dill, lemon pepper, ranch dressing mix, and oil, and they were wonderful in soup and chili. They kept them on hand pretty much all through winter.

He knew Jamie would consider it a treat when he saw them. Right now his plan was to make Jamie as happy as possible. They had some hard things to talk about, and he dreaded the conversation. He got out the ingredients and got the first batch baking while he fixed the other. That still left dessert. Another thing they always had on hand was brownies. Grant knew he couldn't go wrong with that. He decided to run some melted caramels through it with a knife and add some pecan chips.

He was like a mad baker as he whipped one thing up, followed by another. Taking out the last batch of the crackers and setting them out to cool, he put the brownies in to bake and sighed. *Busy, stay busy, don't think.* He started to set the table and thought about putting out settings for four. Grabbing the phone, he dialled a number that had become familiar.

"Officer Johnson, okay, Wade. This is Grant Stevens. Have you had supper yet? Just on your way? Would you like to have supper with Jamie and me? I've made soup and brownies. Yeah, I know it's hot outside. It's a comfort food thing. I'll make a big pitcher of tea. Maybe you can fill us in on any news, anything at all." Grant knew they had to face this and be aggressive in their efforts. Not thinking about it just would not work at all.

"Yes, sir. He's been napping after all the medicine. He was in a lot of pain after all the splinters being removed. Plus, he lost a lot of blood. I'm scared, Wade. I've got to tell you. I'm really getting scared. Somebody is after us again, and the only person I can think of is Donnie. My mind just won't go there. Yes, sir. Anytime in the next hour is fine. It's soup, the longer it sits, the better. Come to the back door. We have something else to show you when you get here." Grant didn't even want to go into the paint on the front porch right now.

Chapter Eleven

Supper was delicious and enjoyed by everyone. Jamie felt better, and it would soon be time for more pain meds so he might even lose the tightness around his mouth. Grant wanted to make it all better. Brit was beside himself, sitting next to Jamie with his head on Jamie's right thigh. He'd stayed close and whined every time Jamie flinched in pain. Grant wanted to join Brit and just sit by Jamie and try to make him feel loved and cared for. But as the brownies made their appearance, he knew it was time for the conversation he'd been dreading.

"Have you found out anything about Donnie, Wade? Would it be unprofessional for you to tell us? Is that why we can't get any information? I don't want you getting into trouble for helping us or for becoming friends with us while you're working on our case. That's not a problem, is it?"

"Not really. It's not the norm, as I've said. But the case was basically over with last year. When we met again this year, it was for something minor and not related, or so we assumed. I just tried again to get some information about

Donnie Wilkins. I got a little more than last time." Wade held his hand up when Jamie and Grant looked at him eagerly

"They seem to be covering up something, there at the prison. No one wants to give me anything on Donnie. I could see that if just anyone called, but since I was on the case last year, it should not be as much trouble as this to find out where he is. I'm getting the captain on it tomorrow. We'll find out something, and I'll get back to you. Now what else did you want to show me?" Taking a last bite of brownie, he stood, and since he was closer to Jamie, he put his hand out to help Jamie up, taking some of the weight off Jamie's sore leg.

They all walked to the front porch, Brit trailing close to Jamie. Flipping on the light they all gathered around the drops of paint that it would seem had been there for a year, unnoticed by them as they went over it time and again. Grant didn't think so.

"Is this from when he painted that crap on your door last year? Or is it the paint you all used to paint the door afterwards? Was it the same colour red that you all used to cover the words he put on it?" Wade bent and put his finger on the biggest spot. He pressed hard to see if it was soft at all. Grant leant over to see if he'd been able to leave a mark on it. He thought the paint was new, that it had been put there recently. It was just one more little mind game someone was playing with them.

Grant watched Wade check the end of his finger and saw that it was dry. They both looked closely at the spot. It hadn't changed. Wade put his fingernail to it and scraped, taking up a bit of it.

"It's pretty dry, but this is fresh paint. If it had been here since last year, it wouldn't have been that easy to scratch up. I'm going to check something," Wade said, taking out a pocketknife and scraping the whole big spot of paint off the porch. He moved over and stuck it to the front door that Grant and Jamie had painted red last year in a rebellious gesture to Donnie, who'd painted an ugly message on it in red paint.

They all moved closer to look at the two colours, and there *were* two colours. It was not the same colour as the door. Grant and Jamie had gotten a little bit darker red colour to cover the mess on the door. This was lighter, more like what Donnie had used to write *Motherfuckin' faggots live here* on their door during his tormenting spree against them.

"Great. One more clue that leads us to believe it's Donnie and not Coach Gilbert. Have you found him yet?" Grant asked, looking from Wade to Mark. Jamie had moved over to the wall by the front door and leant back on it, arms crossed with most of his weight on his right leg.

"We're pretty sure he did go on the fishing trip with a couple of his friends. His wife still seems happy that he hasn't shown up back here. She's probably tired of his behaviour, too. I'm thinking less and less that it's him. I know that leaves us thinking that it has to be Donnie. I promise I'll get to the bottom of this, guys, hopefully before he does anything else."

"Yeah, hopefully," Jamie said, turning to go back inside. Grant was worried about Jamie's frame of mind. This last foray into their own personal madness seemed to have really gotten him down. He needed to do something to lift Jamie's spirits tonight.

They saw off the policemen, their new friends, and locked the front door.

"Hey baby, the guys did a great job after, uh, your fall. They got the whole frame done, and Jim said they'd do the screening and the doors tomorrow. If Wade and Mark come over Friday, maybe you'll feel well enough to join us all outside. Tomorrow, I think we'll take it easy. I'm going to pamper you until you're sick of me."

"Never happen. I need you. I'm having a hard time with this, Grant. I'll admit it. The more it looks like it might be Donnie, the more I get scared that he means to finish what he started last year. I don't know how in the world he could be out of prison, but let's face it. We don't have a lot of enemies. We're just not that kind. Who else could it be?" Jamie had eased down onto the couch in the front room, leaving room for Grant to sit on his right side. Brit settled at the end of the couch, head on his paws.

Grant turned from the waist so he could face Jamie. Raising his hand, he took Jamie's face and pulled it to his. Very softly, he pressed his lips to Jamie's. He took his time, tongue coming out to tease, tickle and lick across the seam of Jamie's mouth. Jamie let him in, never one to keep him out, and their tongues met in a sweet gentle kiss. Right now Grant felt that Jamie needed solace not sex. That was for later, soon, but later. Jamie sighed and moved his face to Grant's neck, turning awkwardly to rest his face into the place where tanned neck met shoulder. Grant let him snuggle in, wrapping Jamie tightly in his arms.

"It's going to be okay. We're not going to be victims this time. We're not. Do you think we should get a weapon? I'm not much for guns, but maybe a couple of Louisville Sluggers, brass knuckles, hell, I don't know. I probably sound like an idiot, but I don't want to be caught somewhere and have him come up on us and there we'd be, like sitting ducks." Grant had never been one to even think about carrying a weapon, and the thought of hitting someone grossed him out, but the thought of one of them being hurt or killed was enough to change his mindset.

"Let's ask Wade what would be the best thing to do. I can handle getting some bats. I think we ought to carry them in the vehicles with us, and one beside each door here. I'm serious. I wouldn't hesitate if I thought he was going to hurt you. I'd brain him in a minute. You know how I feel about you. No one is going to take you away from me." Jamie's voice had gone from quiet and solemn to aggressive.

"I agree with all of that. We need to get smart. I want to find out from Wade where exactly Donnie is. If he *is* out of prison, where's he staying? Surely he has to report to someone like a parole officer or something. I wonder if his dad would know. Have you ever talked to Bob about him?"

"No, we both kind of avoid any mention of him. I know it hit him hard when Donnie went to jail. Finding out all the crimes Donnie had committed to get put away hurt him badly. I feel bad that it all started with some kind of crush or whatever Donnie thought he had on me. The things he did, Grant, the people he hurt. He tried to kill Miss Wilhemina. Oh God! What if he goes after her again or Brit? We've got to do something. He's probably watching us from somewhere. What if he saw her here? He could have followed us when I took her back. How are we going to make sure she's safe?"

"Lord, I hadn't even thought of that. Let's say that tomorrow is going to be information gathering day. We'll let Wade know of our fears for her. I'll go out, seriously, and get four bats. Honest to God, I don't think I could use a gun, but I could whack him with a bat, if I got a chance." Grant looked at Jamie and grinned, ruefully, before adding, "I know in the gun versus bat game, gun wins out, but I have to feel like we're doing something. We're going to put the camera up again, but that would just show him here, not where he's staying. Maybe we could hire someone to try to find him, like a private investigator. He's got to be living somewhere, working, too, if he wants to eat. He's got to be reporting in to someone, too." Grant was still holding Jamie, rubbing his back as his mind clicked over things they could do to take the initiative in this situation.

"Yeah, here we are again. Remember how no one could find him last year? He was able to get around, come around, do all those horrible things, and the police couldn't catch him. I know we can't expect Wade to keep coming when we call every time. We've been lucky so far, catching them when they were available. Let's talk to him tomorrow and see what we can do to protect ourselves and help find him. I'm talking like we know it *is* Donnie. I *think* it is. Don't you?" Jamie pulled his head up, facing Grant again, his expression serious.

"Yeah, I really do. You were right, except for Donnie and Coach Gilbert, I don't think I've ever made anyone really mad. I can't think of anyone who would have it in for me. I know you don't have enemies, either. It's bound to be him. Jesus, that's scary." Grant held on tight to Jamie for a few moments.

"Okay. He's invaded our thoughts enough tonight. Tomorrow we deal. Tonight is all about you. How's the pain? It will be time for more meds soon, so why don't we go get ready for bed. You and I both know it is going to hurt a whole lot more tomorrow, and I doubt if tonight will be a picnic, either. We're leaving the dressing on it for tonight then tomorrow we start with the antibiotic cream and the oil to keep it soft. I'm going to take care of you."

"You always take care of me. You're my guy, huh?" Jamie murmured.

"Yeah, I'm your guy. I know now how you felt last year when I was hurt. It's hard to see someone you love in pain. You were so good to me. Let me help you up." Grant stood and put his hands out for Jamie to grasp. He put his toes to Jamie's and let him pull himself up without too much stress on his leg. Grant saw the grimace Jamie tried to hide, though. He gave Jamie a quick kiss and helped him into the bedroom. Guiding him, Grant took Jamie into the bathroom and propped him up against the counter.

"I have a plan. I know you like to be really clean when you go to bed, and we can't do the shower thing right now, but I think this will work fine and I know that, I for one, will enjoy it. I hope you will, too." Grant leaned in, put his hands on the counter on either side of Jamie's hips, and took another kiss, this one a little longer than the one in the living room. Teasing, he let his tongue move over Jamie's mouth, pushing in, sliding back out, in for more and around for a better taste. Jamie put his arms up and around Grant's neck, pulling him into his body.

"Mmm, this is good, but you're derailing my plans. Just a minute, Jamie, let me get you naked."

"Never been a problem for you," Jamie teased, and Grant's heart leapt. Jamie's demeanour was lightening. He was going to make Jamie feel much better.

"You got that right. You either, for that matter. I think this would best be accomplished if we were both sans clothes. Let me help you get those off past that leg."

Grant eased Jamie's shorts down and made sure they didn't touch his sore leg. He remembered the doctor taking splinter after splinter out of that leg while Jamie gritted his teeth. His poor baby! Grant soon had them naked and both, as expected, were sporting hard eager cocks that Grant intended to take care of shortly.

Turning away, he went to the closet and got out several towels, hand towels, and washcloths. He took a large bath towel and folded it into a wide square and put it on the floor a little closer to the sink than where Jamie currently stood. Motioning for Jamie to step onto it, he put another down for himself in front of the sink. He put another on the side of the counter, pulling Jamie up for a second, then easing him back to rest his cheeks against it. Basically, he was going to wash Jamie, head to toe. The goal was to make it an enticing, sensual experience for both of them.

Jamie kept his mouth shut and watched as Grant got everything ready, reaching into the shower for the shampoo and their favourite soap. He could do this in the shower, but he wanted the mirror and the control this would give him. Not wanting to get the shower going and take a chance on getting the bandage wet, Grant figured this would work and be pretty interesting before it was all over.

"You're working awfully hard there," Jamie teased.

"Plan to. You're my guy, I told you. I've got take care of you. Let's do the hair first. Bend over here, I've got the water just right. You just have to get your head wet. I'll take care of the rest of it. Don't worry about anything getting wet. If the towels don't do the trick, I'll clean it up later. This is just to make you feel good."

Jamie bent and Grant made sure his hair was good and wet, putting a towel around his neck so it wouldn't drip down his back. He got right up in Jamie's face as he put both hands up and massaged the shampoo into Jamie's hair. He moved his hands down to work wonders on the knots in the back of Jamie's neck while he was at it. Tugging and turning him, Grant got Jamie back to the sink and stood to the side and rinsed the shampoo out thoroughly. He covered Jamie's head with the towel and stepped right into his body while he gently rubbed the soft towel over Jamie's hair. Their cocks greeted each other happily and slid against each other in the most wonderful way as he made sure Jamie enjoyed the head treatment.

Stepping back, Grant smiled at Jamie, who was reaching to pull him back.

"Nuh-uh. There's a lot more body for me to work on, and I take my work seriously, you know that. 'Always be thorough' is my motto."

"Is it? I didn't know that." Jamie chuckled, huskily.

"New motto."

"Convenient." Jamie seemed fine with it, though, just fine. Grant stole a glance at Jamie's hard cock, resting on his stomach, the tip leaving a bit of moisture. Yum. Shaking his head at himself, he got back to the task at hand. Getting one of the cloths really wet, he lathered it up, wanting it to be sloppy and wet and leave trails of soapy water running down Jamie's front and back. He'd be careful that none got on that leg, but he was going to make this a wonderful wet wash for Jamie. Then he'd enjoy rinsing the same paths. Drying would be a particular pleasure. He was going to get Jamie settled in the bed, take a quick shower himself and join him, at which point he would, take care of that very hard cock that was just begging for attention.

Grant couldn't take any chances on Jamie falling, or standing for too long or he'd take care of things right now, but he could wait. He set about doing as he planned taking great delight in the shivers as Jamie felt the rivers of water sliding down his back and his chest. Grant made sure to cover every inch of his lover. He even found places where there were still some splatters of blood from the accident this morning. He left no naked spot unwashed from head to toes. He rinsed the cloths over and over and made sure that Jamie was soap free in all areas. The towels were soaking, but doing their job well.

They heard a woof at the door of the bathroom, and Brit stood there looking at them like they were crazy, head tilted. They both laughed, softly.

"Go on and lie down, Brit. Go on, now." Grant told him, smiling when he did.

Finally, Grant dried Jamie, taking great care to be both soothing and sensual at the same time. Moving Jamie's arms, Grant smoothed over them well, sliding his hands down to the pits and grazing them, blowing into them and loving Jamie's laugh at his silliness. He slid the towel over Jamie's chest, taking special care around his tight nipples then down that his flat stomach. Grant made sure the towel didn't hit Jamie's leg while he took a little extra time on Jamie's genitals, teasing and caressing.

Grant urged Jamie to turn and hold onto the counter one more time while he dried his back, buttocks, the backs of his legs and his feet. Done, Grant gathered the towels while he handed toothbrush and paste to Jamie. While Jamie took care of his oral hygiene, Grant took all the towels to the washer since they were so wet. Coming back in, he straightened the bed and turned to find Jamie right behind him.

"That was wonderful, Grant, really. This is the best I've felt since it happened. You do take good care of me. I think I'm ready for some more of that medicine now."

"I figured you would be. You sit here, and I'll get them and a glass of water. Then I think something else needs a little attention." Grant pointed to Jamie's still raging hard on.

"What about you?" Jamie reached for Grant's cock that seemed to be reaching right back for him. Grant stepped back. Not now. Jamie needed pain medicine, now.

"Me, later. Wait here. I'll be right back, promise." Grant hurried for the kitchen to get the pill and the water. He let Brit out for a few seconds, calling him back in quickly after he'd had time to do his thing. He didn't want anything happening to Brit now. Pointing to the corner where his alternate bed was, Grant left him there and headed back to Jamie. Jamie looked as if he were about to fall over just as Grant got there.

"Here, baby. Take this. I don't know how you can be so horny and so sleepy at the same time."

"You're here, that's how. Kiss me."

Grant met his request but didn't linger. He went to his knees between Jamie's legs, liking the gasp from over his head. Putting both hands on Jamie's thighs and moving them apart enough to get his face in between them, Grant got busy. Taking Jamie's cock in one hand and bringing it to his lips, he put the other hand up for Jamie to grasp. For some reason, he knew that Jamie would want the connection with him. Jamie seized his hand and took it to his mouth.

Grant wasted no time getting Jamie off. Jamie needed rest, and this would make him all soft and melty, just what he'd need to sleep well. Grant sucked him in as far as he could and ran his tongue around the tip and down the sides. He slid off and licked all the way down to the base, moving his hand out of the way. He teased the length then took the tip inside for strong suction. Jamie breathed harder and moved his hips, wanting more. He kissed and mouthed Grant's fingers.

Taking Jamie as deeply as he could, he turned his hand around the base, pulling and tugging. Sliding back off it, he provided as much suction as he could and felt Jamie lose it. He grabbed a towel from the stack on the nightstand and cleaned Jamie once more. He kissed Jamie's thighs as he sighed and sort of slumped over towards Grant.

Grant stood quickly, taking hold of Jamie's shoulders. Easing Jamie down so that he was lying flat, he pulled the sheet up and tucked him in, leaning down to kiss him.

"I'm going to take a shower now. You go to sleep. I'll join you in a minute. I'm here for you all night. If you wake up hurting, let me know. Maybe I'll find a way to take your mind off it, or if it's been long enough, I'll get you some more medicine. I love you, Jamie."

"Love...Grant..." That was about all Grant heard, but it was enough.

He turned the lights off and headed for the shower. There, closed in with two doors between them Grant let his tears flow. He'd been there for Jamie all day, strong and confident and ready to take on the world. But now, he had to let the fear and anxiety and adrenaline slide right down the drain with his tears. Good God, what were they going to do now? *Donnie?*

Grant knew the psycho was out to kill them this time. Games were over, and it was full out war. He washed quickly and dried robotically. While brushing his teeth, he looked into the mirror, saw his red eyes and shook his head. Good thing Jamie was already asleep and in the dark. It wouldn't do to let Jamie know how scared he was. Grant talked a good line, but he was scared shitless of something worse happening to Jamie. Straightening his shoulders, he went in to slide in beside his sleeping lover.

It took a while for Grant to drop off.

* * * *

Donnie wasn't wasting time patting himself on the back after the perfect results from last night's efforts. Working quietly, he hid the items he'd bought from the man his last roommate had told him about. This man knew more about explosives than anyone he could imagine, said he'd been in the service until they'd asked him to leave. Didn't matter to Donnie.

Donnie was able to purchase what he needed, and the man had told him how to set it up so both Jamie and Grant would go sky high. Donnie planned on being near enough to see it and far enough away to avoid any fallout, because Grant's pretty new truck was going to blow, big time. He remembered the seller's words.

"Now listen, this stuff is unstable, I'm telling you. It's old, that's why I'm letting you have it cheap. Don't get cocky with it, or you'll blow *yourself* up. Get it in place, carefully, tape it down and when they get going and it shakes up enough, trust me, you'll get the effect you say you want. Keep it in this padded case until you use it, and you better have a steady hand when you do." The guy laughed as Donnie exchanged money for the case. Donnie thought the other man might be just a little crazy.

Donnie walked out of that place with his head held high. His plan was coming together and no one had a clue. He was so proud of the way he'd hoodwinked everyone from the parole officer to the man he worked for each day. They all thought he was a model citizen, changed after his time in prison. He was changed all right. William McDonald AKA Donnie Wilkins was a new man.

Now Donnie just had to wait for the right time. He'd cleared his stuff from the empty house behind where he'd been having fun with his pranks. It had been nice staying there for a little while, cleaning out the pantry and sleeping on such a nice bed. Thinking back over the things he'd done helped him pass the time. He thought the rattlesnake was especially funny. He thought about leaving a dead thing in the washer for the little woman to find, but figured he owed them for the use of their home. Even if they hadn't known they'd offered.

He wanted both men in the truck when the explosion happened, and hopefully that damn dog, too. He was going to get his revenge then he was leaving town. He knew how to hide. He'd proven that. With his knowledge of how to use a new name and a new identity, he'd be fine somewhere far from here. But he wasn't leaving now. He had one more thing to do. His revenge wouldn't be complete until both those men were written up in the obituaries.

Chapter Twelve

The next few days passed in a blur. Men came and worked. Jamie got better, slowly and painfully. The patio and deck were finished, grill and hot tub installed, though Jamie couldn't use it yet, according to the doctor. Soon, though. There had been no more incidents, though neither Grant nor Jamie had let their guard down.

The staff where Miss Wilhemina lived had been advised to stay alert to anyone showing up that they didn't know. They'd promised to take extra care. Jamie and Grant had told Willie about what had been happening and promised to see her as soon as they knew it was safe again. She'd been furious when they'd told her they thought it was Donnie again.

Wade had finally gotten information about Donnie. With his captain's call paving the way, he was able to talk to someone at the prison who knew what had happened. This came only after Wade had explained he believed Donnie was again terrorising the same two men as before and that he'd edged into criminal activity. He told the official some of the things that Donnie had done this time and that was enough to open the floodgates of information.

Wade and Mark showed up at Grant and Jamie's on the Thursday before Jamie had to go back to work on Monday. Wade had called first and not surprisingly gotten an invitation to join them for supper. He swore he hadn't planned it that way, but Grant teased him about it.

Jamie and Grant had decided to eat on the patio. It was nice now that it was screened in with a big whirling ceiling fan moving the air around. Jamie took care of setting the table while Grant finished the meal they'd worked on together. Tonight, they were having one of their favourite summer meals, salad supper. There was a tossed salad with balsamic vinegar dressing, a cold pasta salad with crab meat, peas, and pasta. Grant had even made the now often-requested ramen noodle slaw. He and Jamie had also made a big pan of Rice Krispies Treats.

Once the two officers arrived, greeted Brit first then the two hosts, they all sat down to eat and discuss the situation. Grant felt a little bit as if they were on display, as if they were being watched. He put it down to paranoia, but he was glad Brit was with them. If Donnie was around, he would let them know immediately. After compliments on the food and questions about Jamie's recuperation, Wade got down to business.

"Well, we were all right. It's Donnie." Wade filled them in on how Donnie had managed to arrange early parole. He told them the whole story about the deal he made and that he was out using a different name to protect him from the ones he'd turned on or their friends. Having to report to a parole officer and having a job were part of the deal that had been made and evidently Donnie had kept both promises. As far as the system was concerned, he was doing what he was supposed to do.

"So did they tell you his new name? Is there any way we can find him? Did you tell them what he'd been doing to us?" Grant wanted to know.

"I had to work hard to get this, but I didn't care about the deal they'd made with him, he's on my turf now. I'm real glad those guards lives were saved, but he did that for his own benefit, not theirs. I'm going to meet with his parole officer, an Officer Gann, tomorrow and get more information about him now. I just got this much right before we came over here. I'm sorry it took so long to get this much." Wade shook his head, looking disgusted.

"I hope it won't be like last time when no one could find him," Jamie spoke up.

"Don't remind me. This should be easier. I'll meet with Officer Gann and find out Donnie's current address and where he's working. That'll give us two places to start. What are you doing for Jamie's last weekend off?" Wade asked.

"I'm not sure. Jamie and I talked about going up to the lake again on Saturday. The rest of the time we'll just chill here, I guess. Thank you for keeping us informed and letting us know when you're on. It helps knowing when you're available for help. What did you all do yesterday on your day off?" Grant asked, looking from Wade to Mark, wondering if they'd spent that day together. He'd almost forgotten his earlier feelings that there might be something between them. He watched closely to see if he noticed anything.

Wade looked quickly at Mark, who looked down, and Grant could swear Mark blushed. Grant looked at Jamie to see if he noticed the quick look, and Jamie winked at him.

"We, uh, we were both off so we decided to go fishing out at the pay lake," Wade answered.

"Cool. Did you catch anything? Why aren't we eating fish for supper?" Grant chuckled as they both looked down then burst out laughing.

"Mark's not much of a fisherman, huh Mark? We laughed and told stories and drank cold drinks all afternoon. Tell them about the kid and the cricket, Mark."

"Yeah, Mark, tell us about the kid and the cricket," Jamie and Grant said together then looked at each other, laughing.

"Fine. When I was younger, I worked at a camp for handicapped children in the summers. Each year we had one week that we had really poor kids come in from the inner city of neighbouring areas. We were down at the lake one afternoon, taking them fishing. We gave the kids crickets and taught them how to put them on the hooks. This one kid walked away and took a couple of them and started throwing them against a tree. Over and over, he'd throw the crickets against this tree, very focused."

"That *is* a little weird. What was the deal?" Grant asked.

"I went to him and took his arm and stopped his next throw and asked him what he thought he was doing. His answer blew me away. We laughed and laughed, but when you think about it, it was pretty neat."

"So, what did he say?" Jamie asked.

"He looked up at me, and with this serious face, he said, "You gotta knock 'em out."

Grant and Jamie, and both officers laughed out loud. "You gotta knock 'em out!" Grant said. *How funny.* And how sweet. "Bless his heart," Grant said, "He didn't want to hurt them with the hook so he knocked them out first. That was one smart kid."

"We all thought so. We never fished again without someone telling that story," Mark admitted. "Yesterday was just too hot to enjoy fishing. We just sat in the shade and talked and laughed. Oh, then we went to supper at Catfish Heaven." They all laughed again.

"Let us help you clean up here then we'll go. Have a good weekend and let us know if anything comes up." Mark got up and started grabbing plates. They all did the same and before long the patio was cleared and the dishes done. The officers left, and Jamie and Grant took Brit out for a walk, making sure the house was locked up tight. Strolling down the street in the balmy evening with Brit moving ahead, coming back for a pat every now and then, was very nice.

"I love this area. It's quiet and everyone is friendly. Most people know everyone else, and they watch out for each other. I saw Tony come in earlier. It was nice of him to let me off after your accident. He's a good friend. You think we'll get back to normal soon?" Grant asked Jamie.

Jamie took his hand and they walked on, "Definitely. I'm not accepting anything else. We'll find Donnie and send his ass back to prison where he should stay this time. You about ready to head back? Nice cool shower, nice hot sex, nice long night ahead of us. How about..." Before Jamie could get further in his list of things to come, Brit exploded into furious barking and turning on a dime, started flying back to the house.

Jamie and Grant stood for a second, stunned. They both turned and ran after him, yelling for him to stop, not wanting him to get too far ahead of them and end up getting hurt. Neither could catch him, especially with Jamie limping before they'd gone very many steps. Grant was going to hurry on ahead, but Jamie yelled at him.

"Grant, stop. Don't you go back there without me? We go together. Help me," Jamie reached out for Grant, who stopped and came back to Jamie, putting an arm around his waist. They hobbled as rapidly as possible back to the house where they could still hear Brit barking. When they reached the driveway, Brit was trying to get through the gate into the backyard. Hurrying up to him, they opened the gate and followed him into the yard.

Brit ran straight for the fence, and Grant swore he could see the leaves on the tree moving.

"Jamie, do you see that?" he asked.

"The limb's moving. I'd say we almost caught him in the act this time. You reckon he did anything?" Jamie looked at the deck and patio, wondering if there was any damage evident.

"I don't think he had time. Brit scared him off. Let's call Wade and tell him what happened. Wonder where he, meaning Donnie, goes when he does that?"Grant pointed to the tree limb. "I know the Fines are due back soon. With them gone, he's been using their empty yard to get to us, but where does he go? Does he have a car parked in front of their house? Does he just drive around this neighbourhood like he has the right? The thought infuriates me!"

They were standing by the fence now and Grant wished he could see through it. Was the bastard still over there listening to them? He could be. Brit was still barking.

"Come on, guys. Let's go back in. He's gone for now. We'll tell Wade, but there's no reason for them to come back." Grant took Jamie's arm, steadying him as they headed for the house. "Did you hurt your leg back there? I'll look at it when we go in."

"It'll be all right. It's just sore. I've got another thought before we call Wade," Jamie said as they went up the steps to the patio door. Grant called for Brit, who seemed like he would ignore the call, but finally joined them.

"What are you thinking?" Grant asked him as they headed for the back door. Taking his keys out, he opened the door and let Jamie and Brit enter before locking it back.

"Remember how we didn't think that Coach Gilbert could do the rope trick thing up and over the fence? Well, you knew Donnie. Do you think he could do that? He wasn't fat, but he was really out of shape. I mean it would really take someone who was in great shape to grab a rope and pull himself up and over to the other side of the fence and down, taking the rope with him. Come on, I just don't picture Donnie doing that any more that the coach." Jamie sat down at the kitchen table, his hand rubbing along the top of his leg, which was obviously aching.

"Like someone who's been working out for a year in prison? From what I hear that is about all there is to do. Maybe he's not the same old Donnie," Grant suggested.

"That's it. That's how he's driving around without anyone recognising him. He looks different. Call Wade. I'll fix us a drink. How about some juice?" Jamie asked.

"Sounds good." Grant dialled Wade and filled him in on what happened and what he and Jamie had just discussed. Wade agreed that it could be the case. He said he'd see about getting a picture from the parole officer when he saw him tomorrow. Now they were getting somewhere.

After Grant hung up he asked Jamie what he was going to do tomorrow.

"I think I'll take Brit and go see Miss Wilhemina. I'll be careful and watch for anybody following me. Then maybe

I'll come watch you umpire a couple of games. I think we ought to go to the lake Saturday. We can come back Saturday night and just chill out. I'll get one of those dressings that stick to your skin so I can go in the water. We'll relax and have a good time with Brit. Maybe we'll get this all figured out tomorrow when Wade finds out more about where Donnie is now." Jamie reached for and took Grant's hand, and they headed for the shower to begin on Grant's interrupted list.

* * * *

Behind the fence, Donnie was looking at the camera he'd managed to get down from the corner of the patio. They thought they were so smart, but he was smarter. Been there, done that. They should have known better than to try the same old thing as last year. Boy would they be pissed when they found it missing. Idiots hadn't even noticed it was gone and the damn thing had been in plain sight; especially if you were looking.

He'd heard them making plans. He had what he needed, and he decided that Saturday night would be the perfect time. They'd be tired from the trip and he might be able to get the explosives placed on the bottom of the truck and rigged to blow just like the guy had taught him. Damn near made him hard just thinking about the boom and the body parts flying and then no more pervy boys to think about. Yeah, Saturday night.

* * * *

On Friday, Grant got a visit from Wade while he was in the Parks' main office right after a quick lunch. When he looked up and saw Wade in the doorway, he jumped and hurried over.

"Relax. Nothing has happened. I just left Jamie, and he's fine. I'm here to show you what your nemesis looks like now. By the way, his name is William McDonald."

"How original, from Don Wilkins to Will McDonald! He probably couldn't remember it otherwise. Okay, so show me the picture." Grant held out his hand. Wade put a copy of Donnie's picture in it. Grant stood there, stunned, looking at a thinner, bald, tattooed Donnie. The man looked nothing like he'd looked last year.

"God, he looks, uh…" Grant was at a loss for words.

"Hardened? Like he spent time in prison and learned things while in there?" Mark asked. Grant glanced over at him and nodded.

"So, where does he live and work? Can we just go over there and call him out?" Grant wanted this over.

"Same question Jamie asked and you get the same answer. No. I won't tell you where he lives. But I'll keep an eye on that location and his place of employment. In my talk with Officer Gann, I learned that Donnie's been at work, on time every day, and has never missed a parole meeting. We have no clear evidence right now, but don't think I won't be watching him anytime I'm not on another case. We all know it's him."

"It sucks, knowing he's doing this to us and not being able to do anything about it. I want it over, Wade. You've got how many reports already this time?" Grant's frustration was getting the better of him. "I'm sorry. I know you're doing all you can. Thanks for showing this to me. At least, I'd know him if I saw him now. I don't think

I would have before. Can I have this or will you take it and show it to the people at Miss Wilhemina's place so they'll know not to let him in if he tries to get to her?"

"We'll take care of it. I'll even stop in and see her if they say she's up to it. Stay alert, Grant, and you and Jamie have a good time at the lake tomorrow. I'll swing by your place a few times. We're working the afternoon and evening shift tomorrow. Keep your cell phones charged and with you. We'll stay in contact from now on. Keep it cool, Grant, don't do anything stupid. You don't want to take a chance on being separated from Jamie, do you?"

"Aw now, that wasn't even fair! Cheap, Wade. See when I make slaw for you again." Grant teased him because he knew Wade was right. Neither he nor Jamie was the vigilante type anyway.

"I hear you. But I'm serious, Grant. I don't want you or Jamie doing anything that could put you behind bars. Just live your life and I'll work on this the right way. I'll see you later." Wade turned to Mark and said, "I'm stopping in the bathroom. Too much tea today. Back in a sec." Wade headed over to the men's room, and Grant watched Mark as Mark watched Wade. Yeah, there was something there.

"Uh, if you ever want to talk about anything, Jamie and I consider you a friend, Mark." That's as far as Grant would go. He saw Mark blush and turn back to look at him. Grant tilted his head and looked as earnest as he could. He wanted Mark to know that he could both trust him and talk to him if he needed to.

"I'm pretty transparent, huh? There's not really anything to talk about. It's hopeless. He's straight and therefore, just a friend, you know? He was married before." Mark sounded so dejected Grant found himself wanting to pat his shoulder and tell him things would work out. But he didn't know them that well.

"Don't give up. I've seen him look at you, kinda the same way you look at him. I've never heard him talk about dating women, either. Just be patient, you never know what could happen." Grant wouldn't say any more, but he didn't want Mark to lose all hope.

"Sure. Uh, thanks, Grant. Can you maybe keep this…?"

"Of course, I'm not going to say anything. Hang tough, okay?" Grant said, as Wade motioned for Mark to join him and they left. As soon as they cleared the door, Grant called Jamie on his cell.

"Hey, can you talk? Huh! A minute is all it'll take. Can you believe that picture? That is *so* not the Donnie we knew. I can see this one doing the fence thing, and he looked mean enough to do the rest of it. Scary, Jamie, really scary. Should we leave town tomorrow?" Grant asked. He listened for a moment.

"You're right. He's going to do what he's going to do. Let's get a little break and come back ready to end this thing. Maybe Wade can catch him doing something. Okay, I'll let you go. I have to get back to work, too. Oh, remind me to tell you about my conversation with Mark. Yeah, it was interesting, and kind of what we thought."

Grant spent the rest of the day with visions of the new Donnie in his head, worrying about what the man would do next, who would be hurt, and if there was anything they could do about it. He stopped in Tony's office and filled him in on the latest and told him about their plans for tomorrow. A tentative invitation was issued for Sunday afternoon. He figured Jamie would be up for a cookout with Tony and a couple of the guys who'd helped them build on out back. He wasn't going to stop living his life, just as Wade had suggested.

Chapter Thirteen

They got a late start on their day Saturday because Grant woke up with a hot mouth wrapped around his cock and warm fingers searching between his legs. He spread them accommodatingly and gasped out his pleasure. Moving his hands down, he spread them over Jamie's head and shoulders.

"Jamie, wow. Good morning to you, too. Come here, not by myself. Trade places with me. Come on, turn over and let me get on top. Then we can both get off without you hurting your leg." Grant wanted this to be mutual, and he was still taking care of Jamie.

"Wasn't really ready to stop what I was doing here," Jamie murmured, looking up at Grant with sleepy blue eyes that made Grant's heart turn over. Love for Jamie washed over him as he pushed himself up so he could grasp Jamie's shoulders and pull him up.

"Not stopping, rearranging. I want you, too. Besides, now that I'm fully awake, I want a kiss. I love you. I'm looking forward to our trip today. Let's—"

Kiss. Evidently Jamie was tired of all the talking since he put a stop to it in a most satisfying manner. Grant opened his mouth and let Jamie's persistent tongue inside, meeting it and joining him in an invigorating morning duel.

Jamie pushed him back down and settled on top of him. They'd both realised they loved the feeling of having the other fully lying on them. They were both big guys, and heavy, but the feeling of holding your lover in your arms and feeling his weight pushing you down into the bed was a thrill all its own. Grant had mentioned it to Jamie last year when he'd finally been able to take Jamie's weight after his injuries healed. Jamie had agreed with the comment, and they often indulged in sharing the feeling, often rolling so each could get the rush without being too long on the bottom.

"Ah, you feel so good on me, Jamie. More kissing..."

Jamie was quick to answer Grant's smallest request this morning. Grant sucked on Jamie's tongue then pushed it back into Jamie's mouth, thrusting in and out several times. Soon, they were both breathing hard, and Grant could feel the results of all of their feelings on his stomach. It was time to take this to the next step. He pulled away from Jamie's mouth and pushed against his shoulder so he'd roll over. Grant followed and sat up, turned, and straddled Jamie's body.

His movements put him face to cock and presented Jamie with the same view. They were nearly simultaneous in their next actions. Each took one hand to grasp the other man and soon both cocks were engulfed in hot eager mouths. Grant opened as wide as he could and took Jamie deep inside. He felt the tip of Jamie's cock bump the back of his throat, and he fought the urge to gag. Pulling back just a bit, Grant used his tongue to caress the sides then he pulled off so that the end was just inside his lips. He sucked hard then felt, as well as heard, Jamie's groan. He eased back down the length, using his tongue to flutter around the sides of the warm hard cock.

Grant repeated his movements, going from sucking hard on the tip to teasing all around the length as he took as much as he could inside his hot mouth. Staying focused was hard since Jamie was more or less mirroring his actions between his legs. Jamie was using his other hand to grasp and squeeze Grant's buttocks, sliding a finger down the crack, teasing his hole, then moving to his balls to gently manipulate them. Grant moved his hand to do the same to Jamie since it felt so damn good.

Before long, Grant felt the familiar burning feeling in his balls that heralded the beginnings of his orgasm. He tried not to thrust too hard into Jamie's mouth as he felt the jets of cum bursting forth. Grant didn't want to stop what he was doing to Jamie but was unable to continue for a moment. Jamie was swallowing fast as Grant kept coming. Pulling his mouth off Jamie, he groaned aloud, praising his lover.

"God, Jamie, that's so good. Had to get my breath. Mmm, now, your turn."

He went back to his task and soon was swallowing his lover's cum as Jamie lost it. Grant held on, took it all down and licked and lapped until Jamie was soft and clean. When Grant turned, Jamie looked as if he could go right back to sleep.

"Uh, hello," Grant said, crawling back up to put their heads together. "No sleepyhead today. Saturday, lake trip, Brit, breakfast, up and at 'em, sexy man."

"Well, aren't you wide awake all of a sudden?" Jamie teased him, taking him in his arms and rolling again so Grant was on the bottom again and laughing up into Jamie's face. He wrapped his arms around Jamie's neck and talked into his ear.

"I love you more than I can ever tell you. This is going to be a wonderful day, and I thank you for the wonderful wake-up."

"Love you, too, Grant, more every day. Let's go make this a memory day." Jamie planted a playful kiss on Grant's nose and rolled off and out of the bed. Turning back, he reached for Grant's hand and pulled him out and up beside him.

"If you'll get the shower started, I'll let Brit out and join you. I'll start the coffee, and we can work on getting stuff ready while we eat our nutritious Pop-Tarts."

"Yum. Cherry?" Grant's eyes lit up.

"Of course." Jamie popped Grant's ass as he went by, heading for the bathroom.

* * * *

"Happy, baby?" Jamie's hand on Grant's knee was caressing, moving to his thigh, back up to his knee and squeezing.

"Tired, sweaty and sticky, hungry again, and happier than any man should be. Today was just what I needed. No word from you know who, just you and Brit, good food, good exercise, the lake, and just riding back with you makes me happy. I'm so glad we went. How about you?" Grant asked.

"Ditto to all of that. It was a great day. Well, after the call to Wade to tell him that the camera had been stolen. Gee, wonder who did that? I'm surprised Brit didn't go crazy. Of course, we don't know when he took it, either. I don't look at it every time I go by it. It was lucky you noticed it was gone as we were leaving this morning. Good eye, Grant." Jamie's praise was accompanied by another squeeze on the leg.

"I just happened to glance up there. I couldn't believe it was gone. Wade said they'd come by and look around while we were out. Since he didn't call, I gather he didn't find anything. No surprise there. Donnie's gotten smarter or more careful, at least. Bastard." Grant hated thinking about Donnie, especially today.

"Okay. No more of him tonight. I've had it with him ruining our good times. Let's talk about something else. Back to our wonderful break. I had fun with my two favourite beings on earth," Jamie said, smiling over at Grant.

"I'm glad, baby. Me, too, and I know Brit enjoyed himself. Wasn't he funny?" Grant asked.

"Oh, he had a ball racing us on the beach. I got pretty tired of throwing that stick, but he *was* funny coming out of the water with it, so proud of himself. I'm tired, too, but not too tired to enjoy a shower with you and love you until we're both noodles."

"Noodles?" Grant laughed at Jamie's word choice.

"Yeah, limp and floppy and worn out. We'll sleep well tonight, I promise," Jamie said.

"Oh, I have no doubt. Count me in. You can turn me into a noodle anytime," Grant chuckled and yelped as Jamie squeezed the muscles halfway up his thigh.

"Pasta boy." Jamie was asking for it now.

"I'm not going to be the only one al dente. What are you? Chef Boyardee?" Grant teased.

"Yep, that's me, ravioli, spaghetti, and Grant supreme," Jamie matched Grant's silliness and topped it. They were laughing as they pulled into the driveway. Grant let Brit out and hurried to open the gate for him. Brit liked using his own backyard to do his business, and it had been a long ride home. Grant took a moment to notice that Brit wasn't barking and growling, so maybe Donnie AKA William hadn't been there today. Another reason it was a great day.

"Hey, Brit's not freaking out. Maybe it's been quiet here," Jamie said, matching Grant's thoughts.

"Just what I was thinking. Another reason it was a perfect day. The rest of it sounds pretty good, too. How about bacon, lettuce, and tomato sandwiches for supper? I've got those jumbo hamburger buns and tomatoes big enough to cover them. I'll cook up some bacon if you'll cut some lettuce and we'll be set. That's after the shower, though. I feel grungy."

"Me, too. Sounds good. Let's get this stuff inside first, and we'll get the show on the road. I'm tired, but it's a good tired, you know?"Jamie asked, waiting while Grant opened the back door.

"Yeah, me, too. Here, I'll take the suits to the washer with the towels, and you strip off and leave your clothes there, too. I'll do the same and meet you in the bathroom."

They did the domestic chores and took a short shower filled with touches and glances and kisses that promised a wonderful night of lovemaking to follow. They were soon back in the kitchen and utility room.

"Damn, we're out of detergent. I hate to leave these wet and stinky suits in here," Grant said at the same time, Jamie, from the kitchen said, "Uh, Grant. We're out of

Miracle Whip Light. I don't think I can do BLT's without it. That's like, a necessary ingredient."

"Looks like a quick trip to the grocery. It won't take long. Want me to go? You can stay here with Brit," Grant offered.

"Let's both go. Brit will be fine here. You can head in one direction at the store, and I'll head the other. Maybe we'll stop in the pasta aisle. Suddenly, I'm hungry for spaghetti with homemade meat sauce. We'll be back here in no time. Let's go."

They grabbed wallets, cell phones, the keys and slipped into their tennis shoes by the back door. Brit barked, but Jamie told him they'd be right back. As they stepped out the side patio door and down the steps, Jamie grabbed Grant and put him up against the back of the house.

"What...?" Grant got no more out as his mouth was taken by Jamie's, and he sunk into the hot kiss. *Was it the talk of spaghetti sauce that did it?* Wrapping his arms around Jamie's neck, Grant ground his hips against Jamie's and swallowed the groan the action caused. They stood there for long minutes, kissing passionately and moving their hands over each other.

Finally, Jamie eased back and put his face in Grant's neck. They were both breathing like bellows, gulping in air. Grant smoothed his hands over the back of Jamie's head and neck, calming him, settling him.

"Wow. That was unexpected and just sexy as hell. Don't know what caused it, but I appreciate whatever it was. I've told you before, Jamie Taylor, I love your mouth."

"Mmm," Jamie murmured against Grant's neck. Then Jamie's stomach growled and they broke apart, laughing.

"Guess that's our cue to get going. Come on. Let's get back here quickly," Jamie said, tugging Grant along.

"After that, yeah. Hurrying now." They walked to the gate, went through and stopped dead in their tracks. Was that? *Shit yes*, it was!

"Hey! What are you doing? Get away from my truck!"Grant yelled.

"Damn it, Donnie. Get the fuck out of here. What *is* your problem?" Jamie yelled. Brit could be heard barking inside the house.

Donnie was bent down beside the driver's door. He was on his knees with a box and what looked like a roll of duct tape beside him. They'd startled him and he looked up at them, eyes huge. Jamie and Grant took off running for him, neither pausing to think about danger. There he was! Right there in front of them, obviously getting ready to do something else to Grant's truck.

Donnie grabbed his box and stood quickly, turning and running back down the driveway. He was certainly in better shape than he'd been last year. Then, they could have caught him with no trouble. Now, by the time they got to the end of the driveway, he was in his car, had it started and was pulling away.

"Not this time!" Jamie said then pelted back to the truck. Grant pulled out his phone and punched in Wade's number as soon as he got in the truck.

He'd thrown Jamie the keys naturally, since Jamie still knew the area better than he did, even working for the parks department. There were several parks throughout the county, but he knew Jamie knew all the roads around here as well as Donnie did, and he would have a better time keeping up with Donnie.

Jamie peeled out and sped down the street after Donnie, lips clenched tight.

Finally, Wade answered.

"Wade," Grant yelled into phone while trying to do up his seatbelt. "We just caught Donnie trying to do something to the truck. He saw us and took off, and we're following him. Don't tell me not to. God, Jamie, be careful! We're on Jackson Lane heading out of town. We're not letting him out of our sight. Come on. Wait, let me get my Bluetooth in so I can get Jamie's seatbelt buckled. We're being as safe as we can, but we're not stopping. I want him caught. How far away are you?" Grant asked, finally getting his ear piece in and putting the phone back in his pocket. Now he could talk and have his hands free. He reached for the belt that Jamie pulled out and was holding for him to grab. Punching it into the clasp, he felt better.

"Oh my God, we're in a high speed chase just like on TV. Be careful, Jamie. He's crazy. I don't want anyone hurt here, unless it's him. Where's he going? Out in the boonies?"

"Probably thinks you're driving, and he can lose you out there. Wrong. Tell Wade where we are. Keep him on the line." Both of Jamie's hands were on the wheel and he was intently focused.

"He is. Wade, he is being careful. We're already out of town. We just turned off Meegantown onto Hedly Hill Road. I know it's crooked as hell with steep hills. It's the road the county bus drivers use as a test for when they have snow days. If they can make it up Hedley Hill Road then school is on." They took a curve on what felt like two wheels to Grant. He refused to tell Jamie to be careful again. Jamie was, Grant knew it, but his heart was pumping and adrenaline was making him feel like he was jumping out of his skin.

"It's okay, it's okay. I got it," Jamie said, never taking his eyes from the road.

"Hey, yeah, I can hear you back there." Grant turned to look but couldn't see Wade's police car yet. He glanced over at Jamie, whose gaze was centred on the tail lights ahead of them. Grant felt safe with Jamie driving. Jamie was steady and calm, knowing how to slow for the turns and speed out of them. He kept the same distance from Donnie all the time.

"You're doing good. You're a good driver. Reckon he's just going to keep driving?" Grant asked then wondered if he should just shut up and not distract Jamie.

"He didn't expect us to follow him. He's just driving. I don't think he has a plan. We'll be in the next county in a few miles. Is Wade still on the line?" Jamie didn't take his eyes from the road.

"Yeah, he is. Wade, Donnie had some kind of box and some tape on the ground that he was going to do something with. He took it with him when he ran. I don't know what he had planned, but he wasn't by the gas tank and the doors were locked so we caught him before he could do anything. Yes sir, we'll be careful, but we're not going to let him lose us either. Jamie says we'll be in the next county soon. You can see us?" Grant turned and saw the flashing lights behind them. "Yeah, I see you all. God, this is crazy. Shutting up now."

"Mark's driving." Grant told Jamie. "Damn, that's a steep hill. Jamie, he's going too fast. He's going to miss the curve down there!" Grant held his breath as Donnie's car hit the gravel on the side of the road and fishtailed. He knew his eyes were bugging out of his head as he watched the red tail lights as the car finally straightened up and sped on. Jamie slowed and made the curve safely, then put on speed to catch back up. Now they were going uphill again. Grant felt like he was on the outside seat of a roller coaster going madly up and down and around like crazy. He held on to the 'Oh Shit!' bar over the door and got a good sense of why they called it that.

Grant had just thought it was miraculous that they hadn't met any traffic on the road when they saw lights approaching. Two cars whizzed past them, horns blowing as they went by. Grant watched as Donnie reached the top of the hill, and he held his breath. If he wasn't mistaken, the top of this hill was treacherous as it took a hard right turn at the very top. Jamie sped up, trying to reach the top and not lose Donnie. Grant could see that Jamie had his foot on the brake when he got to the top, knowing he would have to turn. As they got to the top and slowed for the right curve, they realised Donnie wasn't in front of them. Grant rolled down his window, and they heard it.

Donnie's car had left the road when he hadn't slowed enough for the turn at the top. He'd gone right over the edge! Jamie screeched to a stop, and they both jumped out of the truck.

"Wade, Donnie went over the side at the top of Drake's Peak. Yeah, right on the curve. Be careful. Slow down. You can pull over right behind us. We're on the inside of the curve on the edge."

Jamie had waited for Grant to finish, and they both stepped over to the edge. They could still hear the loud sounds of the car still going down the steep hill, through trees and bushes. They saw it roll over and over. The sounds were horrible. The police car pulled up and the doors opened. Grant and Jamie turned to look at Wade and Mark as they stepped out of the cruiser. Just as Wade made it to this side of the car, the ground shook.

Boom!

The last thing Grant saw before he hit the road was Wade and Mark being thrown back against the side of the police cruiser. Grant landed hard on the road, skidding for a bit. His last thought was... *Jamie!*

Grant didn't know how long he lay there in the road before coming to. He raised his head and shook it to try to clear his vision. He was lying near where Mark had parked the car. Wait, the car! Explosion. Now the sound hit him. He could hear and smell fire, and he knew Donnie's car had blown up.

Jamie. Where was Jamie? Grant tried to sit up, but the pain in his head was excruciating. Blood ran down the side of his face. He'd lost his earpiece. His hands were torn up, too. He turned around looking for Jamie, his vision blurring.

There!

Grant tried again to stand, but his legs wouldn't hold him up and his head felt like it was going to burst. He crawled on hands and knees to reach Jamie. As he did, he heard Mark behind him, shouting for Wade.

Touching Jamie on the shoulder, he called to him. His voice sounded funny, muted and slow, like he was underwater. "Jamie. Jamie! Can you hear me? Wake up, baby. Jamie? Come on."

Unlike Grant, Jamie had landed on his back. He was knocked out cold. Grant bent to check for a pulse and breathing sounds. Finding both, he sighed and stroked Jamie's forehead. Oh God, Grant didn't want to think of all the things that could be wrong with Jamie. How hard had he hit his head? Was his neck injured? Jamie looked like he was sleeping, right there on the pavement. His failure to wake up must be because of a head injury and those could be so bad, so bad, so... *don't go there!* Grant tried to shake off his panic and use his own head to take some control of the situation.

"Mark, I can't wake Jamie. Is Wade okay?" Grant turned to look back and saw that both men were standing by the car. Mark was holding Wade up and Wade looked like he might be suffering from a concussion. He wasn't steady and kept trying to push Mark away, but then he would fall back against the car.

"Mark, call for help! See if you can get Wade to sit down for a minute. We need ambulances and the fire department and more help. I can't wake, Jamie! Mark! Please…"

Grant swivelled back to Jamie and realised that they were in the middle of the road. If anyone came from the other direction, they could be run over before they'd even be seen. But he was afraid to move Jamie. What if there was something wrong with his back or his neck? Oh God! What should he do?

"Mark, turn the siren back on so if anyone is coming they'll slow down and see us before they hit us. I'm afraid to move Jamie until I know if he's hurt his back." Grant tried to stand up again and had better luck this time. He was weaving and his legs felt like the noodles Jamie had talked about earlier. Grant didn't want to leave Jamie, but they had to make this a safer spot. Taking a few wobbly steps, he finally made it over to the car where Mark had Wade sitting in the open door of the backseat, sort of rocking but awake.

Mark was on the speaker in the car, asking for all emergency vehicles and giving their location. As soon as he finished, Grant asked, "Do you have any flares in your car? We need to put some way up ahead so no one will drive up on us. From down the hill they'd see the lights, but on this curve and the way we're on the inside of it, I'm afraid they'd be on us before they could stop. Can you do that? I'm afraid to move him. I want to get back to Jamie. He needs me. Jamie needs me." *Okay, Grant you're losing it. Keep it together. You said it, Jamie needs you. Straighten up.*

It hadn't occurred to him to look over the edge. He could hear the fire from the explosion as it ate up trees, grass, bushes and everything on the hillside, getting closer and closer to them. He wasn't worried about Donnie anymore. That was for sure.

Grant made his unsteady way back to Jamie, nearly falling twice, and settled beside him. He wanted to take him in his arms and rock him, hold him, but was afraid it would do some kind of damage to him. It was torture to sit here, not being able to help or even ease Jamie at all. Grant stroked his face, his cheek, touched his lips. He moved his hand down and covered Jamie's heart, feeling the reassuring beat. Thank God, it was strong. Jamie just wouldn't wake up.

"Damn it, wake up, Jamie. You're scaring me," Grant whispered.

"S-sorry."

"What was that? Did you say something? Jamie?" Grant leant over to Jamie's face to see if he'd imagined it. His heart nearly pounded right out of his chest. It was actually painful, but not nearly as bad as his head.

"Shh...hurts." Jamie still didn't open his eyes, but he was awake.

"I know, baby, I know. Me, too. Headache, big time." Grant looked up as Mark came back, also a little unsteady, from placing flares on down the road. They were just visible in the distance.

"Is he awake?" Mark asked, pausing beside them, holding his head.

"Yes. Says he hurts. We know how that feels, huh? We're okay. You go check on Wade. Help will be here soon. I'm glad you were here to call for it."

"They should be here in about five or ten minutes. You're right, I wouldn't move him yet." Mark kept on then, walking slowly to the car and holding onto the top. He leant down to talk quietly to Wade. Grant heard them arguing then both men were walking back to them.

"Stubborn. Couldn't keep him down," Mark muttered as they stopped beside Jamie and Grant.

"What's all that noise?" Jamie muttered, trying to raise his head. "Oh!"

"Yeah, oh! Be still. We have to make sure you don't have a concussion. Hell, I think we all have concussions. Donnie's car blew up. That noise is the hillside burning. Before long, we'll all be crispy critters if help doesn't get here soon. I'm not letting you move 'til we're sure your back or neck isn't hurt." Grant could be stubborn, too.

"Nice thought, but I'm not about to fry. Hold my hand," Jamie ordered. Grant grasped the hand that came up from its resting place on the double yellow line on the road. Jamie held tightly to Grant and it hurt like hell, but he kept hold. Jamie moved first one leg then the other. When he managed both actions with no pain, he moved one upwards until his knee was bent then the other. Success. He then raised his other hand and touched Grant's chin.

"You're bleeding."

"And you're moving. No pain? Everything feel all right?" Grant was thrilled with Jamie's progress.

"Yeah, help me sit up. I'm sure my back is fine, but my head is wobbly and hurts like hell."

"Then you match the rest of us. We should be called the what, Wobbly Warriors? None of us can stand on our feet worth a damn, and I feel like I've been on a three day drunk. And I don't drink!" Wade sounded disgusted.

Grant managed to stand again, and against his better judgement, the three of them bent to help Jamie sit up. He rocked a little like Wade had in the car but soon motioned for them to help him stand.

"We're going to the tailgate of the truck. That's it."

"Good. That's good. That's about all I can make. Not trying to be heroic, but felt kind of funny lyin' on the yellow line there in the middle of the road. Felt sort of like road kill, me and the opossums."

They all laughed at the image but stopped abruptly when it hurt so badly. Grant pulled his tailgate down and they all winced at the sound. All four sat down happily, shaky and spent. It was a tight fit, but they were friends and the experience had bonded them.

"I don't think you all will have to worry about Donnie bothering you anymore,"

Wade said from the end of the row.

"Guess not," Grant said.

"I hear sirens, lots of them. Woo woo," Mark said, his finger circling in the air like the flashing lights. Grant thought maybe Mark was losing it a little, too. Wade snorted at him, trying to laugh but reaching up to hold onto his head instead.

Jamie leaned his head over onto Grant's shoulder and said, "I love you."

"I love you, too," Grant whispered back.

"Aw, isn't that sweet? Mark, aren't they sweet?" Wade said.

"They are. Hell, right now, I love everybody. All those firemen and the polices and the MDT...DMT...EDTs? Shit, who are they?" Yeah, Mark was losing it.

"EMTs," Wade supplied, looking closely at Mark. "You okay, buddy?"

"Fine. I'm fine. You're the wobbly one. I put the flares out there. I'm good, really good. G'night." With that, Mark fell back into the truck in a dead faint. Wade managed to grab the front of his shirt to keep him from hitting his head again.

"Medic! Hey, get some help over here. My partner just passed out. Oh!" Wade grabbed his own head again.

Things happened in a blur after that. Several medical personnel showed up, one for each of them and they were each put on gurneys and into ambulances. The firemen were scrambling all over the hill trying to keep the raging flames under control. It was summertime, hot and dry. This could rapidly turn into a disaster. Grant wished them well.

He knew there'd be an investigation, but that was something to worry about later. Now, he just wanted to get some peace and quiet. Loud yelling and sirens and smoke and headaches just didn't make for a good time. His stomach growled.

Jamie heard it over all that noise from the gurney beside him. "Damn it, we never got our BLTs."

Epilogue

Jamie had gone to get Miss Wilhemina for what she thought was a cookout in honour of her one hundredth birthday. Instead, the yard was nearly full with people, who either knew her or knew of her and wanted to celebrate with her. There were several people from the centre who had worked with her when she'd been with them last year. Some of the guests were from the facility where she was staying now. Most of Grant and Jamie's friends and neighbours were there, including Wade and Mark.

Mark was inside helping Grant with last minute preparations. Tony and Jim were manning the grill, and Wade had a game of horseshoes going in the back part of the yard. The Fines were here, too. Casey was in the game with Wade and Marsha was helping in the kitchen. She was five months pregnant and was sitting at the table, cutting vegetables for a tray with dip.

Grant and Jamie hadn't been too surprised when the Fines had returned from their trip abroad and realised that their home had been broken into. There was a mess in the some of the rooms and a lot of food was missing. Donnie hadn't bothered to clean up after himself and the odour had hit them as they'd entered the house. They'd found that the back door had been jimmied and the alarm turned off. No one was sure how he'd done that without the company coming by, but it had taken a while before they were ready to move in again. Grant and Jamie had apologised profusely as they'd felt it was their fault.

"They should be here any minute. We should have someone watching for them so we can all be outside when she comes through the gate. Bless her heart. She thinks she's all alone. Well, except for Jamie and me. She'll be so surprised to see so many people here for her. I can't believe how well she is doing for a woman of her age. She's able to get around with just a cane and her mind is clear. That blows me away." Grant went to the back door and motioned for one of their neighbour's kids to come over. He asked the teenager to watch for Jamie's car so they could all be ready when Willie arrived.

After the night of the crazy car chase, as Grant and Jamie referred to it, they had tried to spend time at least once a week with Willie. She kept insisting they call her that! They had taken her out to lunch a couple of times, waiting on her at a local buffet where she loved the old fashioned cooking. She'd been to the house several times, and each time, she demanded the right to help with something for the meal. After two of the visits they had found that she had somehow managed to leave them a note without them seeing her writing it.

You've brought such joy into my life. Love, Willie.

To Grant (Handsome) and Jamie (My Sweet Boy): The love I feel in this house is contagious.

Needless to say, these were treasured notes and in the drawer with the others, minus the one that Donnie had written, of course. Often Willie sat in a recliner with Brit by her side. Her hand was always moving over him, patting, rubbing, and her voice was soft as she told him how special he was.

Grant and Jamie had gotten a huge sheet cake with the inscription "*Wilhemina. Celebrating one hundred years of a lovely life.*" On one corner at the top was a yellow icing square that had a note from Jamie and on the other corner was one from Grant. Written on the notes were words from each of them.

Jamie's note said, "*Brit and I consider you an honorary grandma. We love you. Jamie.*" Beside Jamie's name was a paw print. Grant's note read, "*I'm so happy to be part of your family. Love, Grant.*" It was a beautiful cake with fall colours and leaves on it.

The weather was unseasonably warm for November, in the seventies, so they were having the party outside. They'd put her favourite recliner out on the patio where she would be protected from the sun and heat. They planned to seat her like a queen and let her enjoy the festivities in her honour. No one had brought gifts, at their request, for what did you give someone of her age who had no home of her own? They knew she would appreciate that. Just the party would have her in what she called happy tears.

At the warning from the young man they'd sent to watch, they all headed out to be in the yard when she arrived. Grant had the camera ready for her reaction. Most of the vehicles had been parked in neighbour's drives along the street so the surprise should be genuine. Grant could hear Jamie talking with her as they neared the gate. The gate opened and Brit came through first, barking as if to herald her entrance.

When she appeared in the open gate, as rehearsed, everyone in the yard started singing, "Happy Birthday, Miss Willie."

Grant, through the zoom lens, could see the shock on her face and the tears that formed as the song progressed. Jamie had a good hold on her so she wouldn't falter and Brit stood by her other side. Her hand was on his head, as if she needed something familiar to keep her grounded.

After taking several shots, Grant handed off the camera and headed over to embrace Willie. He walked right up to her and took her into his arms.

"Happy birthday, Willie. I hope you enjoy your party. There are lots of people here to wish you the best." Grant could feel her shaking in his arms. He drew back to make sure she was all right.

"Hi, Handsome. What have you boys done? Oh, my goodness gracious. All of these people can't be here for me!" She looked back and forth from Grant to Jamie, and when they both smiled and nodded, she took a deep breath and said, "Well, I hope there's a cake." Everyone burst into laughter at that.

Grant gave a signal, and soft music began from speakers on the patio. Grant and Jamie had worked hard making a couple of CD's that were full of songs from the thirties to the sixties.

Jamie and Grant escorted Willie to her seat and the party began. Several of their friends had become hers too, from all the cookouts she'd been to here. Grant returned to the kitchen to finish getting things ready for supper. He heard laughter from outside so he knew things were going great.

The cake was a big hit, and Willie proudly cut the first pieces and insisted that Grant and Jamie take them. They got her a piece and the three of them sat together at a table and talked together. Grant kept a close eye on her to make sure she wasn't getting too tired. She seemed fine, but that might be adrenaline.

"Are you getting tired, darlin'?" he asked, reaching out to touch her hand.

"I'm gloriously tired and happy and thrilled. I can't believe you all went to all this trouble for me." She looked at them both then shook her head and said, "What am I saying? Of course, I can believe it. This is the kind of people you are. You've taken a lonely old lady and made her a family member. That is priceless. You all are the light of my life. I never expected to have such joy in my life at this age. Now, how silly did that sound? I never thought I'd be this age, but you all have made it wonderful. I can never thank you enough."

"We love you, Willie. We do feel like you're part of our family and we're lucky to have you in our lives." Grant put his hand on his chest and said in an exaggerated voice, "You complete us."

"Oh my, Handsome, you are so funny. Don't think I don't remember that movie. I do."

Brit had his head lying on Willie's lap, and Jamie was sitting close to her. He put an arm around her and leant over to kiss her cheek. She blushed prettily and reached to brush his face. Grant could see the love between the two of them, and it touched his heart like it always had.

"Okay, boys. I think it's time to take me back, and I'll take a nice nap. If you don't mind, I'll take a piece of that cake to have tomorrow. After I'm gone, you can put on some music that won't bore your guests. I enjoyed hearing all those songs so much."

"Oh, we forgot to tell you. We have you a small boom box and the CD's are for you to take with you. You can listen to them whenever you want and think about all the people who love you and think you are the cat's meow. Isn't that a term from your era?" Jamie asked.

"Yes, dear boy, it is. You all have done your homework for this. I love you dearly. Let's go, now, before I start to cry again. I can't thank you enough. You, too, Brit. You are my special love, aren't you?" She bent to kiss Brit's nose. He licked her chin, and she giggled like a school girl.

Grant fixed her a plate with two pieces of cake on it and added a couple of plastic forks and napkins. He put it all in a basket that had her musical gift in it. He hugged her and walked out with them. In a last surprise for her, everyone had a candle and Wade and Mark had gone around the yard, lighting them all. When Jamie and Grant stepped out the door of the patio with her, everyone turned with their lit candles and began to sing, softly and quietly, "You light up my life…"

The three paused to listen for a few minutes as the group sang about lighting up her days and filling her night with song. She had both hands up to her mouth as she looked all around the yard. It was beautiful and just perfect as far as Grant was concerned. He felt pride in how well things had gone off.

"Thanks, guys," he yelled, and they turned to escort her to Jamie's car. Grant kissed her goodbye and returned to the party while Jamie took her back to her home. What a wonderful day. What Jamie didn't know was that Grant had a wonderful night planned for them, too. Well, as soon as everyone left.

As expected, the music had changed and now the Black Eyed Peas were getting things going as the crowd started thinning. Some guests were leaving and others were staying around for a while. He found that most of the mess had been cleaned up, and Wade and Mark were inside with Tony putting things away and washing the last of the dishes.

"Hey guys, you all didn't have to do that. But thanks. You all want to stay and play cards after everyone else leaves? Mark, we still owe you for kicking all our butts at Phase 10." Grant wouldn't mind at all if they stayed and played for a while. His plans for Jamie did not have a time frame, and he knew Jamie enjoyed spending time with his friends.

Tony begged off and said he had some reports to work on that he'd put off all weekend. Wade and Mark said they'd stay until Jamie got back and see if he wanted to play for a while. With the kitchen in good shape, they trooped out to see who was left and what was going on. The few people still there were gathered together and chatting about things in general. No one mentioned Donnie, his campaign of terror or his death. Frankly, it had been talked to death, and Grant was glad it was no longer a part of either their conversation or their life.

Jamie returned and the conversation continued. The success of the party was toasted with bottles of sparkling grape juice, one of Jamie's favourites. A little later, it was down to the four of them, and they were indeed playing cards, good natured ribbing and teasing throughout the game.

Wade and Mark had become good friends and since they were no longer part of any case, they didn't have to worry about it being against anyone's definition of professional behaviour. Now they were just friends. Grant and Jamie still noticed that Mark was all but wearing his heart on his sleeve. While Wade seemed to be unaware of it, there were times Grant thought he saw a look in Wade's eyes as Wade looked at Mark.

Grant thought it would be wonderful if the other couple became, well, a couple. Not once in all the times they'd been together had Wade ever mentioned seeing or being interested in women. Anytime they planned an evening or an outing together, it was always the two of them that showed up together. They were almost a couple already. Grant wished only the best for them. He wanted everyone to be as happy as he and Jamie were.

"Oh! Not again! Mark, you have to be cheating," Jamie teased as once again Mark went out first.

"Don't have to. You all just have something else on your mind, and you're not paying attention to who's saving what. I don't know what Wade's excuse is," Mark answered, smartly.

"Keep on. I'll get you back," Wade promised.

"Bring it," Mark replied, eyes bright.

"Ooh, Jamie. You think they're gonna arm wrestle?" Grant asked, teasing.

"Maybe they should," Jamie said, looking from Wade to Mark, laughing.

"Fine," Wade said. "I'm game. You up for it?" he asked, looking at Mark.

"As I said, bring it," Mark said, looking eager and excited.

They scooted their chairs around and place their arms on the table, raised, ready to grasp hands. Grant stood back a little, but between them and dropped his hand in a sign for them to begin. Muscles strained in both arms as Jamie did a low-voiced doo-doomp, doo-doomp, doo doomp, sounding like the music from the movie Jaws. Grant nearly burst into laughter at the silliness of it. He watched the determination on both men's faces as they gripped hands tightly and each tried to force the other's hand down. Grant would always say that Mark threw it as his hand was slowly but surely put down to the table by Wade.

Surprisingly, Wade didn't gloat with his victory. There was a weird vibe in the air, one almost of anticipation. With few words, the two men left, and Grant and Jamie were alone. They stood at the back door and heard Wade say, "Hey Mark, wait up. Do you want to…?" Grant and Jamie looked at each other and smiled.

"Why is it we want them to get together so much?" Jamie asked, tilting his head and looking at Grant.

"Because we want them to be as happy as we are and we think that being together would make them so. But, it's up to Wade. I know Mark is ready, but it remains to be seen if Wade is able to admit how attracted he is and how much he cares for Mark. It's out of our hands. We'll just be here to support them both, no matter what happens with them," Grant said, ducking his head as he realised how wise he sounded.

"You're right. Come here," Jamie said, pulling Grant into his arms. "It was a good day, and I think Willie was really surprised and happy. It felt good making her feel loved and honoured. Being that smart and healthy at her age is a hell of an accomplishment. We did good." Jamie ended his little speech with a kiss on Grant's lips and firm, rocking hug.

"Oh, it's not completely over yet. Didn't you know? There's more planned for later...which is, frankly, right now." Grant pulled away from Jamie and took his hand, leading him towards the bedroom, turning out lights on the way. With a firm point, he sent Brit to the bed in the kitchen corner by the utility room.

"Oh, I like a man with a plan," Jamie said, following obediently. "Can I help?"

"Certainly. See how quickly you can get undressed and meet me in the middle of the bed."

"You got it." In seconds, Jamie was on the bed, naked, arms extended. Perfect. Grant disrobed and met him there in just as few seconds.

Grant slid over to lie beside Jamie, on his side, head propped on his hand.

"Do you know how much I love you? Talk about lighting up someone's life. One thing I've learned this year is not to take happiness for granted. It could be taken away at any time. I don't want you to ever doubt how much I love you and want you in my life forever." He leaned the small bit needed to place his lips on Jamie's waiting ones. Jamie put his hand up and cupped the back of Grant's neck, holding it still while he lengthened the kiss, tracing Grant's lips and teasing the corners.

Grant moved closer, dropped his pose and settled into Jamie's body. Placing one hand on Jamie's shoulder, the other moved over his stomach, heading downward. Grant opened his mouth to accept Jamie's questing tongue and felt the zing of excitement run straight to his groin. He moved his hardening cock against Jamie's, and at Jamie's urging, he moved over until he was lying on top of Jamie.

He lined them up so that any movement provided friction for their cocks, now nestled together.

"Forever," Jamie managed to get out once he moved his head a bit, looking up into Grant's eyes. "That's what I want with you, too. I love you, Grant, love, love, love you. You're my guy."

"I'm your guy, forever, Jamie."

"So, what's the rest of your plan?" Jamie asked, hips pushing up, making their cocks slide against each other in a very satisfying manner. Grant pushed right back in an action-reaction move that brought a groan from Jamie.

"'Your choice night' is what I'm calling it. What would you like to do, Jamie? I'm here to make your night as perfect as I can." Grant put his face down into Jamie's neck and moved his lips nibbling, nipping and sliding against the skin where Jamie's shoulder met his neck, knowing it was sensitive.

"Yeah? Tonight, what I would like is for you to make love to me. I want to watch your face while you do. I want you to fill me up then lean down and kiss me hard. I want to feel all of you. I want your hands on me when I come. Then I want to hold you all night long." Jamie tugged Grant's head up to look at him as he finished his list of requests.

Grant smiled down at Jamie and said, "I think I can make every bit of that come true."

"Good. When's it 'your choice night'?" Jamie asked, pulling Grant's lips down to his.

"Tonight."

About the Author

AKM Miles loves reading the M/M genre and decided to write what she loves. Early authors, read years ago in this area, were not as much interested in love, storyline, and character development, as those that she has found recently. Thrilled with the new works, AKM set out to make a career in this field. You can expect there to be a happy ending every time. You can expect for the two to find each other and choose to be together fairly early on, and then face conflicts, trials, and experiences as a couple. AKM prefers that over going back and forth over whether the love is returned or not. She loves to throw children in the mix, along with pets and wacky and wonderful friends. Hopefully, readers will love the emotional love stories that fill her head and spill onto her computer.

AKM Miles loves to hear from readers. You can find her contact information, website details and author profile page at http://www.total-e-bound.com.

Total-E-Bound Publishing

www.total-e-bound.com

Take a look at our exciting range of literagasmic™
erotic romance titles and discover pure quality
at Total-E-Bound.